PENGUIN BOOKS

PACO'S STORY

Larry Heinemann was born and raised in Chicago. He served a tour of duty with the 25th Division in Vietnam as a combat infantryman. *Close Quarters*, his award-winning Vietnam novel, has been called *the* seminal work to come out of that war. C. D. B. Bryan called it, "The best book by anyone who fought there." Penguin Books has recently issued a paperback edition, and a worldwide Dutch-language edition was published in 1986.

His shorter fiction has appeared in *Harper's*, *Penthouse* (as part of their Peabody Award–winning Vietnam series), and *TriQuarterly*, as well as *The Best American Short Stories of 1980*, *The Best of TriQuarterly*, the recently published *Soldiers and Civilians*, and elsewhere. His nonfiction has appeared in *Harper's*, the *Chicago Daily News*, and the *Chicago Sun-Times*. Mr. Heinemann has received literature fellowships from the National Endowment for the Arts and the Illinois Arts Council.

Mr. Heinemann lives in Chicago with his wife, Edie, and their two children. He is currently working on a nonfiction book about posttraumatic delayed stress and the "tripwire" veterans of the Olympic Peninsula and the Pacific Northwest.

"Read *Paco's Story.*

It's a piece of work. There may be novels that are longer, slicker, smoother, glitzier—but none of them can match the deep psychological truth of *Paco's Story.*"

—Asa Baber, *Chicago Sun-Times*

"Resonates with a devastating and bitter irony. . . . Heinemann writes about the workingman's Vietnam, exceptional for its bleak, shared, unexceptional reality. This is the war, no question, and there is no escape."

—*The Philadelphia Inquirer*

"This second novel by the author of the critically acclaimed *Close Quarters* is likewise a very frightening, yet wondrously rendered tale of violent extremes of human behavior. A strongly emotional reading experience . . . Highly recommended"

—*Library Journal*

"*Paco's Story* is eerie, powerful, and convincing."

—Tracy Kidder, author of *House*

"*Paco's Story* deserves a place among the best Vietnam war novels."

—*Providence Sunday Journal*

"Do not read *Paco's Story* unless you are prepared to find yourself bitterly wanting to cry. The tears, if they come, will be for the ghosts of Vietnam. *Paco's Story* is brave and terrible."

—*Atlanta Journal-Constitution*

"More than a tale of war, *Paco's Story* is an examination of suffering and redemption, penitence and atonement, with salvation available only to those who recognize the unending human capacity for viciousness."

—*Bergen (New Jersey) Record*

LARRY HEINEMANN

PACO'S STORY

PENGUIN BOOKS

PENGUIN BOOKS

Viking Penguin Inc., 40 West 23rd Street,
New York, New York 10010, U.S.A.
Penguin Books Ltd, 27 Wrights Lane, London W8 5TZ
(Publishing & Editorial) and Harmondsworth,
Middlesex, England (Distribution & Warehouse)
Penguin Books Australia Ltd, Ringwood,
Victoria, Australia
Penguin Books Canada Limited, 2801 John Street,
Markham, Ontario, Canada L3R 1B4
Penguin Books (N.Z.) Ltd, 182–190 Wairau Road,
Auckland 10, New Zealand

First published in the United States of America by
Farrar Straus & Giroux, Inc., 1986
This edition with a foreword by the author
first published in Penguin Books 1987

Parts of this book first appeared, in slightly different form, in *Harper's*
magazine (1980, 1981) and *TriQuarterly* (1979, 1984)
Lyrics from "Wild Horses" (page 114) written by Mick Jagger and Keith
Richards © 1970 ABKCO MUSIC, INC. (BMI). Reprinted by permission. All
rights reserved
The author thanks the Illinois Arts Council and the National Endowment
for the Arts for their support during the time this book was being written

LIBRARY OF CONGRESS CATALOGING IN PUBLICATION DATA
Heinemann, Larry.
Paco's story.
1. Vietnamese Conflict, 1961–1975—Fiction.
I. Title.
PS3558.E4573P3   1987   813'.54   87-8687
ISBN 0 14 01.0085 7

Printed in the United States of America by
Offset Paperback Mfrs., Inc., Dallas, Pennsylvania
Set in Primer

For Edie, my wife,

and for Sarah Catherine

and Preston John

Foreword: A Word to the Reader

The "James" comes from the custom of street folks engaging total strangers by calling them "Jim" or "Jack" or sometimes "Jake" in a jivy sort of way—if you were looking for directions or exact change for the bus or a light for your smoke, say. But since Paco's story requires language more formal than street-corner patois, I thought "James" more apropos. I also had in mind the tongue-in-cheek punch line "Home, James." When I first began working on the story, a good friend asked me whether "James" was in fact James Jones—a writer whose work I greatly admire (and think is vastly underrated); he died of a painful and lingering illness just before my first novel was published, in 1977. I told my friend that, no, "James" was *not* James Jones, but the coincidence was too powerful an irony to ignore and dismiss.

But as it turns out, there are many "Jameses." There are two disciples named James: Saint James the Less (brother or cousin of Jesus of Nazareth and considered to be the author of the epistle in the Bible) and Saint James the Greater. There are six King Jameses of Scotland and two of England, including James I, who commissioned the Authorized (or King James) Version of the Holy Bible. There are the literary "Jameses"—James Joyce, Henry James, his brother William James, and James Jones among them. And we can include the legendary outlaw Jesse James, his brother Frank James, and the James Gang; James Bowie, killed along with every other man at the Battle of the Alamo (his brother made him the famous hunting/fighting knife that bears his name); and the actor James Dean, whose personal legend helped to define the post–World War II era.

Further, James is the name of my oldest brother—a man I have not seen or heard of since 1970 or thereabouts. And, finally, my father's name was John, though everyone called him Jack—sometimes a nickname for James; he died not two weeks before the publication of my first novel, *Close Quarters*, which made that a paradoxical and contradictory event, indeed —exhausted grief accompanied by exhausted relief.

—*Larry Heinemann, 1987*

Contents

Then I heard a loud cry in our own language

and it said: "Do not touch me! I am Crazy Horse!"

BLACK ELK, *Black Elk Speaks*

Paco's Story

1/13/88

Pat —
God bless +
take good care.

[signature]

1. The First Clean Fact.

Let's begin with the first clean fact, James: This ain't no war story. War stories are out —one, two, three, and a heave-ho, into the lake you go with all the other alewife scuz and foamy harbor scum. But isn't it a pity. All those crinkly, soggy sorts of laid-by tellings crowded together as thick and pitiful as street cobbles, floating mushy bellies up, like so much moldy shag rug (dead as rusty-ass doornails and smelling so peculiar and un-Christian). Just isn't it a pity, because here and there and yonder among the corpses are some prize-winning, leg-pulling daisies—some real pop-in-the-oven muffins, so to speak, some real softly lobbed, easy-out line drives.

But that's the way of the world, or so the fairy tales go. The people with the purse strings and apron strings gripped in their hot and soft little hands denounce war stories—with perfect diction and practiced gestures—as a geek-monster species of evil-ugly rumor. (A geek, James, is a carnival performer whose whole act consists of biting the head off a live

3

chicken or a snake.) These people who denounce war stories stand bolt upright and proclaim with broad and timely sweeps of the arm that war stories put *other* folks to sleep where they sit. (When the contrary is more to the truth, James. Any carny worth his cashbox—not dead or in jail or squirreled away in some county nuthouse—will tell you that most folks will shell out hard-earned, greenback cash, every time, to see artfully performed, urgently fascinating, grisly and gruesome carnage.)

Other people (getting witty and spry, floor-of-the-Senate, let-me-read-this-here-palaver-into-the-*Congressional-Record*, showboat oratorical) slip one hand under a vest flap and slide one elegantly spit-shined wing-tip shoe forward ever so clever, and swear and be *damned* if all that snoring at war stories doesn't rattle windows for miles around—all the way to Pokorneyville, or so the papers claim. (Pokorneyville, James, is a real place, you understand, a little bit of a town between Wheeling and Half Day at the junction of U.S. Route 12 and Aptakisic Road—a Texaco gas station, a Swedish bakery, and Don't Drive Beddie-Bye Motel.)

And a distinct but mouthy minority—book-learned witchcraft amateurs and half-savvy street punks and patriots-for-cash (for some piddling hand-to-mouth wage, James)—slyly hang their heads and secretly insinuate that the snoring (he-honk, he-honk, the way a good, mean, shake-shake-like-a-rag-doll snore snaps at you, James) is nothing if it isn't the Apocalypse itself choking on its own spit, trying to catch its breath for one more go-round.

And the geeks and freaks and sideshow grifters of this world hear the dipstick yokels soaking up a shill like that, well, damned if they don't haul off a belly laugh—haw haw haw. *They* know a prize-winning shuck when they hear one, James.

4

They lean back in their folding lawn chairs, lined up in front of their setups and shacks—the Skil-Thro and Ring Toss and Guess-How-Many-Pennies-in-the-Jar-Bub? and such as that— and slap their thighs hard enough to raise welts, all the while whispering among themselves that the rubes of this world will *never* get the hang of things.

Now, according to some people, folks do not want to hear about Alpha Company—us grunts—busting jungle and busting cherries from Landing Zone Skator-Gator to Scat Man Do (wherever *that* is), humping and *hauling ass* all the way. We used French Colonial maps back then—the names of towns and map symbols and elevation lines crinkled and curlicued and squeezed together, as incomprehensible as the Chiricahua dialect of Apache. We never could cipher a goddamned thing on those maps, so absolutely and precisely where Scat Man Do is tongue cannot tell, but we asked around and followed Lieutenant Stennett's nose—flashing through some fine fire-fight possibilities, punji pits the size of copper mines, not to mention hog pens and chicken coops (scattering chickens and chicken feathers like so many wood chips). We made it to the fountain square in downtown Scat Man Do—and back to LZ Skator-Gator—in an afternoon, James, singing snatches of arias and duets from *Simon Boccanegra* and *The Flying Dutchman* at the top of our socks. But what we went there for no one ever told us, and none of us—what was left of us that time —ever bothered to ask.

And some people think that folks do not want to hear about the night at Fire Base Sweet Pea when the company got kicked in the mouth good and hard—street-fight hard—and wound up spitting slivers of brown teeth and bloody scabs for a fortnight. Lieutenant Stennett had us night-laagered in a lumpy, rocky slope down the way from high ground—his first (but by no stretch of your imagination his last) mistake. And you could hawk a gob of phlegm and spit into the woodline from your foxhole, James. And it was raining to beat the band. And no one was getting any sleep. And just after midnight—according to Gallagher's radium-dial watch—some zonked-out zip crawled up sneaky-close in the mangled underbrush and whispered in the pouring rain, "Hey, you! Rich-chard Nick-zun is a egg-suckin' hunk of runny owlshit!" And then Paco and the rest of us heard him and some other zip giggling—tee-hee-hee-hee—as though that was the world's worst thing they could think to say, and would provoke us into rageful anger. But before any of us could wipe the rain out of our eyes, Jonesy raised his head from his rucksack, where he was taking one of his famous naps—fucking the duck, we called it—and stage-whispered right back, "Listen, you squint-eyed spook, you ain' tellin' me annathang ah don' know!" Then they whispered back at us with one voice, as giggly and shivery cute as a couple smart-ass six-year-olds, "GI, you *die* tonight!" and then giggled some more. Paco blinked his eyes slowly, glancing out of the corners as if to say he didn't believe he heard what he *knew* he heard, and shook his head, saying out loud, "What do these zips think this is, some kind of chickenshit Bruce Dern–Michael J. Pollard–John Wayne movie? '*GI, you* die *tonight!*' What kind of a fucked-up attitude is that?" Then he leaned over his sopping-wet rucksack in the direction of the smirking giggles, put his hands to his mouth, megaphone-fashion, and said, "Hawkshit," loud enough for the whole company to hear. "Put your money where your mouth is, Slopehead," he said. "Whip it on me!"

So later that night they did. They greased half the 4th platoon and Lieutenant Stennett's brand-new radioman, and we greased so many of them it wasn't even funny. The lieutenant got pissed off at Paco for mouthing off and getting his radioman blown away so soon—but that was okay, because the lieutenant wasn't "wrapped too tight," as Jonesy would say.

The next morning we got up, brushed ourselves off, cleared away the air-strike garbage—the firefight junk and jungle junk —and dusted off the walking wounded and the litter wounded and the body bags. And the morning after that, just as right as rain, James, we saddled up our rucksacks and slugged off into the deepest, baddest part of the Goongone Forest north of our base camp at Phuc Luc, looking to kick some ass—anybody's ass (can you dig it, James?)—and take some names. Yessiree! We hacked and humped our way from one end of that god-damned woods to the other—crisscrossing wherever our whim took us—no more sophisticated or complicated or elegant than an organized gang; looking to nail any and all of that god-damned giggling slime we came across to the barn door. Then one bright and cheery morning, when our month was up, Private First Class Elijah Raintree George Washington Carver Jones (Jonesy for short, James) had thirty-nine pairs of black-ened, leathery, wrinkly ears strung on a bit of black commo wire and wrapped like a garland around that bit of turned-out brim of his steel helmet. He had snipped the ears off with a pearl-handled straight razor just as quick and slick as you'd lance a boil the size of a baseball—snicker-snack—the way he bragged his uncle could skin a poached deer. He cured the ears a couple days by tucking them under that bit of turned-out brim of his steel helmet, then toted them crammed in a spare sock.

The night that Lieutenant Stennett called it quits, Jonesy sat up way after dark stringing those ears on that bit of black wire and sucking snips of C-ration beefsteak through his teeth.

And the next afternoon, when we finally humped through the south gate at Phuc Luc, you should have seen those rear-area motherfucking housecats bug their eyes and cringe every muscle in their bodies, and generally suck back against the buildings (you would have been right proud, James). Jonesy danced this way and that—shucking and jiving, juking and high-stepping, rolling his eyes and snapping his fingers in time —twirling that necklace to a fare-thee-well, shaking and jangling it (as much as a necklace of ears will jangle, James) and generally fooling with it as though it were a cheerleader's pom-pom.

And the Phuc Luc base camp Viets couldn't help but look, too. Now, the Viets worked the PX checkout counters (good-looking women who had to put out right smart and regular to keep their jobs), the PX barbershop (where the Viet barbers could run a thirty-five-cent haircut into $6.50 in fifteen minutes), and the stylishly thatched souvenir shack (where a bandy-legged ARVN cripple sold flimsy beer coolers and zip-a-dee-doo-dah housecat ashtrays, and athletic-style jackets that had a map embroidered on the back with the scrolled legend *Hot damn—Vietnam* sewn in underneath). And, James, don't you know they were Viets during the day and zips at night; one zip we body-counted one time couldn't booby-trap a shithouse any better than he could cut hair.

Every Viet in base camp crowded the doorways and screened windows, and such as that, gawking at Jonesy—and the rest of us, too. So he made a special show of shaking those ears at them, witch-doctor-fashion, while booming out some gibberish mumbo jumbo in his best amen-corner baritone and laughing that cool, nasty, grisly laugh of his, acting the jive fool for all those housecats. And the rest of the company—what was left of us *that* time—laughed at him, too, even though we humped those last three hundred meters to the tents (up an incline) on sloppy, bloody blisters, with our teeth gritted and the fraying rucksack straps squeezing permanent grooves in our shoulders. (A body never gets used to humping, James. When the word comes, you saddle your rucksack on your back, take a deep breath and set your jaw good and tight, then lean a little forward, as though you're walking into a stiff and blunt nor'easter, and begin by putting one foot in front of the other. After a good little while you've got two sharp pains as straight as a die from your shoulders to your kidneys, but there's nothing to do for it but grit your teeth a little harder and keep humping. And swear to God, James, those last uphill three hundred meters were the sorriest, goddamnedest three hundred motherfuckers in all of Southeast Asia. Captain Courtney Culpepper, who never missed a chance to flash his West Point class ring in your face—that ring the size of a Hamilton railroad watch—never once sent the trucks to meet us at the gate: said we had humped that far, might as well hump the rest.)

Nor do people think that folks want to hear what a stone bore (and we do mean *stone*, James) sitting bunker guard could be. Now some troopers called it perimeter guard and some called it berm guard, but it was all the same. The bunkers, James: broad, sloping sandbagged affairs the size of a forty-acre farm on the outside and a one-rack clothes closet inside, lined up every forty meters or so along the perimeter, within easy grenade range of the concertina wire and the marsh. You sit scrunched up, bent-backed, and stoop-shouldered on a plain pine plank, staring through a gun slit the size of a mail slot. And you stare at a couple hundred meters of shitty-ass marsh that no zip in his right mind would try to cross, terraced rice paddy long gone to seed, and a raggedy-assed, beat-to-shit woodline yonder. (That woodline was *all* fucked up, James; because we used to shoot it up every now and again out of sheer fucking boredom.) Well, you stare at all that, and stare at it, until the moonlit, starlit image of weeds and reeds and bamboo saplings and bubbling marsh slime burns itself into the back of your head in the manner of Daguerre's first go with a camera obscura. You peep through that skinny-ass embrasure with your M–16 on full rock and roll, a double armful of fragmentation grenades—frags, we called them—hanging above your head on a double arm's length of tripflare wire, and every hour at the quarter hour you crank up the land-line handphone and call in a situation report—sit-rep, we called it—to the main bunker up the hill in back of you fifty paces or so. "Hell-o? Hell-o, Main Bunker!" you say, extra-friendly-like. "Yez," comes this sleepy, scrawny voice, mellowed by forty meters of land-line commo wire. "This here is Bunker Number 7," you say, and snatch one more glance downrange—everything bone-numb evil and cathedral-quiet. "Everything is okeydokey. Hunky-dory. In-the-pink and couldn't-be-sweeter!" And that sleepy, scrawny voice takes a good long pause, and takes a breath, and drawls right back at you, "Well, okay, cuz!"

And between those calls up the hill—and taking a break every now and again to take a whiz, downrange—you have nothing better to do than stare at that marsh and twiddle your thumbs, and give the old pecker a few tugs for the practice, wet-dreaming about that Eurasian broad with the luscious, exquisite titties who toured with a Filipino trio and turned tricks for anyone of commissioned rank.

Those Filipinos, James, they were extra-ordinary. One guy played a rickety Hawaiian guitar, one guy played a banged-up tenor saxophone, and the third guy played the electric accordion—and that dude could squeeze some *fine* accordion, James. That trio and the woman played every nickel-and-dime base camp, every falling-down mess hall and sleazy, scruffy Enlisted Men's Club south of the 17th Parallel (the DMZ, we called it)—as famous in their own way as Washing Machine Charlie, the legendary night rider of Guadalcanal. So how come they never made the papers, you may ask.

Well, James, reporters, as a gang, acted as though our whole purpose for being there was to entertain them. They'd look at you from under the snappily canted brim of an Abercrombie & Fitch Australian bush hat as much as to say, "Come on, kid, *astonish* me! Say *something* fucked up and quotable, *something* evil, something *bloody* and *nasty*, and be quick about it—I ain't got all day; I'm on a deadline." But mostly you'd see them with one foot on the lead-pipe rail and one elbow on the stained plywood bar of the Mark Twain Lounge of the Hyatt-Regency Saigon, swilling ice-cold raspberry daiquiris and vodka sours by the pitcherful—pussy drinks, bartenders call them. The younger, "hipper" ones popped opium on the sly or sprinkled it on their jays, and chewed speed like Aspergum, but their rap was the same, "Don't these ignorant fucking grunts *die* ugly! It's goddamned *bee-utiful!*" They'd lean sideways against the bar, drugstore-cowboy-style—twiddling their swizzle sticks—and stare down at their rugged-looking L. L. Bean hiking boots or Adidas triple-strip deluxe gym shoes,

swapping bullshit lies and up-country war stories. "Say, Jack,"
would say this dried-up, milky-eyed old sports hack from the
Pokorneyville Weekly Volunteer-Register, "I seen this goofy,
wiggy-eyed, light-skinned spade up at Fire Base Gee-Gaw las'
week. Had some weird shit scrawled on the back of his flak
jacket, Jack: 'Rule 1. Take no shit. Rule 2. Cut no slack. Rule 3.
Kill all prisoners.' I ast him if he was octoroon—he looked
octoroon to me—and he says (can you beat this?), 'I ain't
octoroon, I'm from Philly!' Haw-shit, buddy-boy, some of these
nigras is awful D-U-M-B." Then slush-eyes'll take another
couple he-man slugs of raspberry daiquiri, smacking his lips
and grinning to high heaven.

So, James, listening to conversation like that, how can
anyone expect reporters and journalists—and that kind—
would appreciate anything as subtle and arcane and pitiful as
one three-piece USO band and the snazziest, hot-to-trot honey-
fuck to hit the mainland since the first French settlers. Those
guys can't be everywhere, now, can they?

Those Filipinos ha-wonked and razza-razzed and pee-
winged, sharping and flatting right along for close to three
hours down at the lighted end of our company mess hall. The
whole charm of their music was the fact that they couldn't hit
the same note at the same time at the same pitch if you passed
a hat, plunked the money down, put a .45 to their heads, and
said, "There! Now, damnit, play!" They played the "Orange
Blossom Special" and "Home on the Range" and "You Ain't
Nothing but a Hound Dog" and "I Can't Get No Satisfaction,"
after a fashion. And they played songs like "Good Night, Irene"
and "I Wonder Who's Kissing Her Now" and "I Love You a
Bushel and a Peck"—music nobody ever heard of but the gray-
headed lifers. And that woman, who hardly had a stitch on

(and she was one fluffy dish, James), wiggled pretty little titties
right in the colonel's mustache—Colonel Hubbel having himself a front-row kitchen chair—and she sure did sit him up
straight, *all right*. And the rest of the battalion officers and
hangers-on (artillery chaplains and brigade headquarters busy-
bodies on the slum) sat shoulder patch to shoulder patch in a
squared-off semicircle just as parade-ground pretty as you
please. They crossed their legs to hide their hard-ons, and tried
to look as blasé and matter-of-fact—as officer-like and gentle-
manly—as was possible, trying to keep us huns away from the
honey. And the rest of the company, us grunts, stood close-
packed on the floor and the chairs and tables, and hung, one-
armed, from the rafters—our tongues hanging out, swilling
beer from the meat locker and circle-jerking our brains out.
Our forearms just a-flying, James; our forearms just a blur.
And that broad shimmied and pranced around near-naked,
jiggling her sweating little titties like someone juggling two
one-pound lumps of greasy, shining hamburger, and dry-
humping the air with sure and steady rhythmic thrusts of her
nifty little snatch—ta-tada-ha-humpa, ta-tada-ha-humpa, ta-
tada-ha-humpa, *ha-whoo*! Then a couple black guys from the
3rd platoon's ambush began to clap their hands in time and
shout, "Come awn, Sweet Pea, twiddle those goddamn thangs in
my mustache! Come awn, Coozie, why don't ya'll sit awn *my*
face—yaw haw haw."

(Let's tell it true, James, do you expect we'll ever see that
scene in a movie?)

But most particularly, people think that folks do not want
to hear about the night at Fire Base Harriette—down the way
from LZ Skator-Gator, and within earshot of a ragtag bunch

of mud-and-thatch hooches everyone called Gookville—when the whole company, except for one guy, got killed. Fucked-up dead, James; scarfed up. Everybody but Paco got nominated and voted into the Hall of Fame in one fell swoop. The company was night-laagered in a tight-assed perimeter up past our eyeballs in a no-shit firefight with a battalion of headhunter NVA—corpses and cartridge brass and oily magazines and dud frags scattered around, and everyone running low on ammo. Lieutenant Stennett crouched over his radio hoarsely screaming map coordinates to every piece of artillery, every air strike and gunship within radio range, like it was going out of style, when all of a sudden—*zoom*—the air came alive and crawled and yammered and whizzed and hummed with the roar and buzz of a thousand incoming rounds. It was hard to see for all the gunpowder smoke and dust kicked up by all the muzzle flashes, but everyone looked up—GIs *and* zips—and knew it was every incoming round left in Creation, a wild and bloody shitstorm, a ball-busting cataclysm. We knew that the dirt under our bellies (and the woods and the villes and us with it) was going to be pulverized to ash (and we do mean *pulverized*, James), so you could draw a thatch rake through it and not find the chunks; knew by the overwhelming, ear-piercing whine we swore was splitting our heads wide open that those rounds were the size of houses. We don't know what the rest of the company did, or the zips for that matter, but the 2nd squad of the 2nd platoon swapped that peculiar look around that travels from victim to victim in any disaster. We ciphered it out right then and there that we couldn't dig a hole deep enough, fast enough; couldn't crawl under something thick enough; couldn't drop our rifles, and whatnot, and turn tail and beat feet far enough but that this incoming wouldn't catch us by the scruff of the shirt, so to speak, and lay us lengthwise. We looked around at one another as much as to say, "*Oh fuck! My man, this ain't your average, ordinary, everyday, garden-variety sort of incoming. This one's going to blow everybody down.*" Swear to God, James, there are those days—no matter how hard you hump and scrap and scratch—when there is simply nothing left to do but pucker and submit. Paco slipped off his bandanna and sprinkled the last of his canteen water on it, wiped his face and hands, then twirled it up again and tied it around his neck—the knot to one side. Jonesy laid himself out, with his head on his rucksack, getting ready to take another one of his famous naps. Most of the rest of us simply sat back and ran our fingers through our hair to make ourselves as presentable as possible. And Gallagher, who had a red-and-black tattoo of a dragon on his forearm from his wrist to his elbow, buttoned his shirt sleeves and brushed himself off, and sat cross-legged, with his hands folded meditatively in his lap. In another instant everyone within earshot was quiet, and a hush of anticipation rippled through the crowd, like a big wind that strikes many trees all at once. Then we heard the air rushing ahead of those rounds the same as a breeze through a cave— so sharp and cool on the face, refreshing and foul all at once— as though those rounds were floating down to us as limp and leisurely as cottonwood leaves. We looked one another up and down one more time, as much as to say, "Been nice. See you around. *Fucking shit!* Here it comes."

And in less time than it takes to tell it, James, we screamed loud and nasty, and everything was transformed into Crispy Critters for half a dozen clicks in any direction you would have cared to point; everything smelling of ash and marrow and spontaneous combustion; everything—dog tags, slivers of meat, letters from home, scraps of sandbags and rucksacks and MPC scrip, jungle shit and human shit—*everything* hanging out of the woodline looking like so much rust-colored puke.

Yes, sir, James, we screamed our gonads slam-up, squeeze-up against our diaphragms, screamed volumes of unprintable oaths. When the motherfuckers hit we didn't go *poof* of a piece; rather, we disappeared like sand dunes in a stiff and steady offshore ocean breeze—one goddamned grain at a time. We disappeared the same as if someone had dropped a spot of dirt into a tall, clear glass of water—bits of mud trailed behind that spot until it finally dissolved and nothing reached bottom but a swirling film. (Not that it didn't smart, James. Oh, it tickled right smart. First it thumped ever so softly on the top of our heads—your fat-assed uncle patting you on your hat, leaning way back and bragging his fool head off about how proud he is of the way you do your chores. But then came the bone-crushing, ball-busting rush—the senior class's butter-headed peckerwood flashing around the locker room, snapping the trademark corner of a sopping-wet shower towel upside everyone's head with a mighty crack. Whack!)

Whooie! We reared back and let her rip so loud and vicious that half a world away all the brothers and sisters at Parson Doo-dah's Meeting House Revival fled—we mean *split*, James; we mean they peeled the varnish off the double front doors in their haste. The good parson was stalking back and forth in front of the pulpit rail, shouting and getting happy, slapping his big meaty hands together, signifying those sinners—bim-bam-boom—and calling on the mercy of Sweet Jesus. Well, sir, our screams hit the roofing tin like the dictionary definition of a hailstorm and swooped down the coal-stove chimney—"Ah-shoo!" Those sinners jumped back a row or two as though

Brother Doo-dah had thrown something scalding in their faces. They threw up their arms, wiggled and wagged their fingers, shouting to high heaven, "Alle-lujah!" "A-men!" "Yes, Lord!" "Save me, Jesus!" Then they grabbed their dog-eared Bibles and hand-crocheted heirloom shawls, and hit the bricks. Yes, sir, James, plenty of the good brothers and sisters got right and righteous *that* night. And Brother Doo-dah was left standing in the settling dust slowly scratching his bald, shining head, pondering—wondering—just exactly how did he do that marvelous thing?

Oh, we dissolved all right, everybody but Paco, but our screams burst through the ozone; burst through the rags and tatters and café-curtain-looking aurora borealis, and so forth and suchlike; clean as a whistle; clean as a new car—unfucked-with and frequency-perfect out into God's Everlasting Cosmos. Out where it's hot enough to shrivel your eyeballs to the shape and color and consistency of raisins; out where it's cold enough to freeze your breath to resemble slab plastic.

And we're pushing up daisies for half a handful of millennia (we're *all* pushing up daisies, James), until we're powder finer than talc, *finer* than fine, as smooth and hollow as an old salt lick—but that blood-curdling scream is rattling all over God's ever-loving Creation like a BB in a boxcar, only louder.

2. God's Marvelous Plan.

Our man Paco, not dead but sure as shit should be, lies flat on his back and wide to the sky, with slashing lacerations, big watery burn blisters, and broken, splintered, *ruined* legs. He wallows in this greasy, silken muck that covers him and everything else for a stone's throw and dries to a stinking sandy crust. He lies there that night and all the next day, the next night and half the second day, with his heels hooked on a gnarled, charred, nearly fire-hardened vine root; immobile. And he comes to consciousness in the dark of that first long night with a heavy dew already soaked through the rags of his clothes, and he doesn't know what hit him.

'Am *I* ever fucked up, he thinks to himself, but he doesn't so much say this or even think it as he imagines looking down at his own body, seeing—vividly—every gaping shrapnel nick, every puckery burn scar, every splintery compound fracture.

And at first he concentrates his whole considerable attention on listening—for the cries, the hoarse, gulped breathing, the whispering supplication of the other wounded, for water, for Jigs the medic, for God's simple mercy. (Swear to God, James, you have not heard anything in this life until you have heard small clear voices in the dark of night calling distinctly, "Help me, please"—though they say the crying of wounded horses is worse.) Paco waits with closed eyes and stilled breath, to shiver and be appalled at the dry raspy voices; waits patiently to whisper back in answer. But he hears, of course, nothing.

So he lies there, nearly motionless because of the pain—ticking like a living thing, until he comes to understand it as a living thing, as if some small animal with bristling, matted fur had crawled up to him for warmth—and he stares, marveling, into the black and distant, vaulted heavens, his vision blurred by blood-spattered dust. The next morning the sun rises, quickly burning off the misted dew, and slantingly strikes his face, but he cannot raise his arm out of the muck to cover his eyes, cannot turn his head aside. And all that hot, bright day the sun shines in his eyes as sharply as salt, and the tears of that bitter, crushing pain stream into his hair, and his scalp itches powerfully. By the middle of the afternoon he is covered with bugs drawn by the stench—big black deerflies and tiny translucent maggots, small gnats with bites like hard mean pinches, which immediately become stinging welts, raw and infected, drawing pus at the least touch.

Paco lies there virtually stock-still all the second night and half the second day, burning with fever and as good as delirious. And Bravo Company (which doesn't have so much as a pot to piss in nor a window to throw it out of), and their young and skinny, exhausted medic, come looking for what is left of Alpha Company, and they don't find Paco until nearly noon, and he is only barely alive.

The Bravo Company medic who finds Paco will tell the story of it (this years later) in Weiss's Saloon, over and over again. It will be late afternoon. A clear north light will come in the large store-front windows, with their water-spotted sills crowded with potted geraniums, African violets, and tall, spiny coleuses. The light will catch the metal edges of the tables, the curved tops of the bentwood chairs, and will spread a fine sheen on the scuffed plank floor. The medic, older and rounder and more shabby-looking, sits slouched, leans back in one of the creaking chairs and eats ice-cold hard-boiled eggs (each bite dipped in salt and hot mustard). All that afternoon and evening he will drink mug after mug of beer with shots of whiskey or schnapps—boilermakers—and he will drink them hard.

"We were in the bushes for two solid months, *that* time, up around the Goongone Forest," the medic will begin, slurping at some foam. "And every fuckin' day for the first nineteen days it's me dusting off KIA, killed in action, dead guys, you understand? and wounded, too. We were getting contact every day good and steady," the medic will say every time he tells it, taking a moment to drop a whiskey, shot and glass and all, into his beer. "Tracking an NVA company they fuckin' tell us, and guys're dropping like flies, Jack—horrible fuckin' heat exhaustion, ordinary ambushes, sniper fire, Chicom claymore mines as big as tractor tires, dumb-fuck firefight heroes. Guys with their heads cracked open like walnuts, bleeding from the ears and the scalp. Guys with their chests squashed flat from fuckin'-A booby-trapped bombs. Guys with their legs blown off

20

at the thighs, and shrapnel hits from there on up from a direct hit with a Chicom RPG—an armor-piercing rocket-propelled grenade. Shit! Mean and evil blood all over everything and *my* ass in it up to the elbows. I still dream about it nights—nightmare monsters that smell to high heaven, nasty whirligig-looking contraptions that keep snatching at you, slobbery-looking warlocks with the evil fuckin' eye that gives you cold sweats and shivers so bad you think you got some dynamite dose of malaria.

"After a while the company gets up in the morning, *every* fuckin' morning, and waits for the motherfucker to settle somewhere. Some days we never had to leave our night-laager. Ka-blamo, some poor fuckin' fool would get his eating breakfast—there it is, Jack, nothin' left of him but his plastic spoon. I'd wrap the sons-a-bitches up and shoot them up, whispering, 'Naw, you ain't gonna die,' you poor dumb fucker. '*Trust me!*' and they'd smile right back at me, 'Thanks,' like they really believed that *bull*shit line, and then their eyes would roll back into their heads ('Thanks'), and their heads would roll back on their shoulders ('Thanks'), and they'd pass out from shock and die before the dust-off medevac chopper could haul-ass out to us. And the captain would be having one of his famous conniption fits, screaming some gibberish nonsense into the radio; then he'd get pissed and throw the microphone down and kick it, and he'd throw his hat down and kick *it*. 'These goddamn people are holding up this whole fuckin' war!' he'd say, meaning the dust-off choppers.

"And sometimes the dust-off came in time, but that wasn't no fuckin' guarantee. We'd load the dude up and ten minutes later the captain would get some half-garbled radio message that the guy was DOA—dead on arrival—croaked halfway there. And you'd be standing there waiting, just hating to hear it. The captain'd call me over and have a shit fit reading me the riot act, complete with bugged eyes and bloody foam at the mouth from his bad gums. He was *definitely* crazy.

"One KIA a day, Jack, every fuckin' day," the medic will say, and shake his head at the bartender. The bartender will put a mug to the tap and pull. "Morning, noon, *and* night. Fuckin'-A.

"Then one night we're listening to Alpha Company doing it hot and heavy, and they were getting down and getting some, but then ka-bar-room-*room-room-room!* This incredible fuckin' noise—I mean I've heard incoming, but *that* must have been the all-time prize. We got a radio message from Colonel Hubbel to check it out, he can't get Alpha Company on the radio. The captain got up. 'Shit!' he said. 'Why can't that miserable old fart get off his own dead ass for once and hop his fuckin' chopper and do it himself. And why can't he pick on somebody else for a change. All right, everybody get up!' he said, 'Let's go,' and went around kicking at people.

"The captain was antsy anyway, a real eager beaver when you got right down to it—looking for his Purple Hearts and his medals—so we saddled up and started off in the middle of the night. Well, fuckin' goddamn, we got about two hundred meters downrange when the point squad stepped right in the motherfucker—a three-man ambush that we just buried in this shitstorm of frags. But we had one KIA and two wounded. The cap got all pissed off and had another shit fit, and we didn't get going again until after daybreak. We thrashed around in that fuckin' woods—the Goongone Forest, you understand— that night, the next day, the next night, and *that* day. And we were *always* lost. Son-of-a-bitch, Jack, there were more dumb fucks in Bravo Company than anywhere. The cap would flip open this bullshit company compass he had and sight it on the company map, gawking at the numerals on the dial, and thinking to himself, What is this goddamn gizmo? Some kind of chickenshit Cracker Jack prize? He would bang it against his leg, like it was waterlogged and maybe *that* would help. Then he'd have another shit fit, kicking stumps and throwing food, but then he'd take a drink of water and simmer down, and we'd proceed."

The medic will carefully crack the hard-boiled eggs, then twist the shells carefully back and forth so that they're rendered nearly in two.

"Well, finally, late in the morning of the second day we found Fire Base Harriette and what was left of Alpha Company, which wasn't much more than a smell I couldn't begin to compare with anything I've smelled since. There was nothing there, Jack, not even the village or that old French fort, just this one guy, *that* poor dumb bastard. Alpha Company got wiped out. The whole company, except for this *one* cat, caught some mean kind of shit and every swinging dick *but* him bought the motherfucker. So, why ain't he dead? He had a fuckin' day and a half. Why ain't he bled to death? Why ain't he shriveled up with heatstroke like a piece of dried-up bacon? That whole place stank to high heaven. *He* stank to high heaven. I often wonder why we didn't just keep fuckin' walkin'. A bunch of us stood where we jolly well knew the command bunker should have been—*everybody's* pulled time at Harriette, you understand. We took one good look around us—no bunkers, no trenches, almost no woodline—and knew we weren't going to find enough of those sorry motherfuckers to fill a dozen peck baskets." The medic will lean back in his chair and look up at the bartender, who listens for the hundredth time, blandly looking around his bar and counting the chairs the medic has emptied.

On that day at Harriette the captain (a robust and thoughtful man, James, but astonished and enraged, bewildered and infuriated by his continuing bad luck, irritated to distraction) stood with the medic and the radioman and the others near the command bunker, teetering on a chunk of timber, with his thumbs hooked on his rucksack straps—that rucksack crammed as full and piled as high as any rucksack in the company. He gazed around at the carnage and the wreckage—shivers of gooseflesh rising in him like a fever— and all the while he thought to himself, This is a mean and ugly way to die and a rotten goddamn fucking piece of luck to be sure, and God forgive me, but thank the sweet and holy Blessed Virgin Mary, Queen of Heaven, Mother of God, at least *this* time it ain't me and mine.

"And when we found that guy who survived that shitstorm," the medic will say, resuming, brushing bits of egg yolk out of his mustache, "he was piping hot and still pouring sweat, mumbling gibberish and crying. He wasn't wearing his dog tags like he was supposed to, so God only knew who he was. But why he wasn't dead is anybody's guess. *I* didn't know, and I didn't want to know. He looked up at me, trying to be friendly somehow or other. And he knew he was fucked-up royal. It didn't take no genius. His legs were so torn up, like someone would snap twigs for kindling, that the sons-a-bitchin' dust-off medics slipped him into a spare body bag to save everything but his asshole—though he still had his cock and his balls, you understand. And the rest of him looked like someone had taken off after him with one of those long-handled mallets you tenderize meat with.

"Anyway, I took one good long look at the guy, flies and bugs on him so thick he was a blur, Jack—fuzzy. And I've fuckin' had it."

The young medic stood with the captain and the rest, staring down at Paco, and a wave of saddening disgust went through him that drained the blood from his face, and he was revolted, defeated.

"I turned to the other company medic, this conscientious objector—a fuckin' new guy—said, 'Fuck this, Jack, or whatever your name is, *you* do it. I'm goddamn sick and fuckin' tired of these sons-a-bitches dying on me. I ain't gonna eat this shit anymore. I quit . . .'"

But the conscientious objector fumbled and grab-assed, nervous and humiliated, and generally made such a muddle of it that the first medic finally pushed him aside and finished, applying what aid he could, tourniquet and all. He asked Paco questions, speaking hoarsely, "Who are you? What happened here? Who *are* you? What the fuck happened?" But all Paco did was cry steady tears—his mouth watering with hot tears. The medic waited, slumping over him, until the dust-off chopper came, wiping Paco's blackened, sun-blistered face with a water-soaked shirttail that stung Paco's cheeks and felt gritty and raw on his stiff and bleeding lips.

When the dust-off came skidding in on the fly and settled into the crusted muck of Fire Base Harriette, first ankle-deep and then shin-deep, the dust-off medics glanced down at the Bravo Company medic with a quick and pitiful look. He watched the chopper medics (wearing o.d. T-shirts and spiffy

trousers, and clean, well-tended jungle boots) slip Paco gingerly
into a body bag up to his waist. He helped a couple of Bravo
Company troopers tote the litter, and helped secure the litter
to the open rack in the chopper. Then he turned and walked
back to his rucksack and aid bag, his boots crunching in the
crusted slime as though it were a frozen field of blizzard snow.
The dust-off rose barely inches off the ground, hovering, then
nosed down—dipping forward with a long sweep—and moved
off, making speed and altitude surely. The chopper medics
stood next to Paco's litter, trying to soothe his hoarse, hysterical
crying as best they could, and looked out and down at the
smooth sandy ground and the bare heads and bare backs of
the Bravo Company troopers as they went about picking up
the pieces of combat-loss equipment and gear, collecting scraps
and chunks of the corpses in body bags. The chopper circled
wide of Fire Base Harriette and over the jungle out of the
smell, barely skimming the woodline trees, making them billow.
As the chopper swept along, the medics picked bugs and jungle
junk out of Paco's wounds firmly and precisely, thinking to
themselves, At least it isn't a *dozen* guys—the floor smeared
with blood and that bloody jungle stink in their clothes and hair
and mustaches all goddamn day.

The two Bravo medics hovered around the radio, expecting to hear that our man Paco died on the chopper—why
should the twentieth sorry son-of-a-bitch be any different?
Exhausted and numb and suffocatingly hot, aching with anticipation, the medic fully expected to hear that everything but
the Alpha Company man's asshole got blown away in the
breeze, like so much bloody confetti, what with the chopper
pilot hauling ass hell-for-leather, the way they did, back to the
evacuation hospital, with the doors of the chopper as wide

open as a ditch sluice. In his mind's eye, the medic would always imagine the dust-off medics pissing and moaning for days after about the blood slopped all over the inside—though there was little—remarking among themselves about that poor dumb fucker from the Alpha Company holocaust surviving all *that* shit *and* two days' exposure, and "was he ever a fucking mess." And *then* when the best part of him blows away in the chopper rotor wash—the medic clearly imagining this, too— he hears them grumble, side-mouthed, "Ain't gonna bet on this guy. Won't make it much past the triage, you ask me. He'll be pushing up daisies by suppertime, sure."

That night in the claustrophobic privacy and quiet of the darkness (in a steady monsoon downpour, with every man in the company sitting sullen and sleepless, and the medic glanc- ing at the radio every now and again, expecting to hear, *still*, of the death of that Alpha Company man—the waiting really *galling* him now), the medic suffered a heart attack. There were sharp and sustained, gripping chest pains, stuttered breathing, a tingling numbness down his left arm and that side of his face, and a shockingly severe and prolonged acute short- ness of breath. And he gasped and grimaced and puzzled over it—that pain as if someone had reached in and was *squeezing* his heart—but then he himself guessed it, a heart attack of all things, a thrombosis; how do you figure that?

And the next morning, in the bright, hot light of day, with the monsoon clouds clearing away to the west, the medic rose, stretched, and yawned (with the overwhelming nausea of the thrombosis still rising in him powerfully), and he looked around, sour-faced, at the carnage and the ruin, the wreckage, at his fellows in Bravo Company (Which one of them will die today?). And, James, it was as if he saw the sheer, manifest ugliness—the blunt and pervasive, raw and stupefying ugliness—of that place for the first time. And he was suddenly, finally, ready to admit that no matter what he did or how much, it was never enough; no matter how hard or neat he worked—grim and earnest—the wounded always died (you can only tie a tourniquet so tight, James; you cannot give a stomach wound any water; you cannot give a head wound any morphine). Standing there stripped to the waist, with his low-slung, wringing-wet trousers and wool socks clinging to his pasty, clammy skin, he suppressed the heartsick upwelling of tears. He walked toward the middle of the encampment to a shallow, soupy puddle, then squatted down in the muck, reached between his knees, and skimmed up handful after handful of water—creamy with ash and silt—and pressed his hands to his face, slapping and pulling at it the way drunks do. He scooped his hands deeper and deeper (the silt running out between his fingers), and squeezed them into fists, even pushing his knuckles together for leverage, until all he had left were two tight little knots of moist dirt, smelling of that peculiar odor of corpses.

(And the medic, sitting at the table at Weiss's Saloon, James, will suddenly open his hands and slap them, knuckles down, flat on the table and stare at the yellow calluses and the lines of his palms—impregnated with grease. He will always remember those small gray lumps the shape of the inside of tight and powerful fists, and he will imagine the smell from all those corpses rising into his face, like the steady heat from a kitchen oven.)

He dropped the knots of dirt back into the creamy puddle, stood up, and walked away. And without telling anyone of his heart attack—stiff-necked and stoic about his still-souring nausea—the medic gathered up his soaking-wet aid bag and rucksack, and went straight to the captain to turn in his time.

The captain stood eating a C-ration can of bread—a heavy and solid, floury and tasteless lump about the size of a muffin, James, packed into a small green tin can—and shared a canteen cup of heavily chlorinated water with three or four other men (the water so bitter with iodine you could spit all day long and still not get that metallic, medicinal aftertaste out of your mouth). The other troopers saw the medic coming at the captain and turned away, knowing without saying that he'd come to talk, man to man. And when the medic got three paces from the captain he tossed the aid bag at the man's feet and started right in as best he could: "I quit. When that fuckin' chopper comes, I'm leaving, and you can't fuckin' stop me. I ain't comin' back and you can't make me. I'd rather do hard time at LBJ," the medic said, as if he'd rehearsed it, and looked right at the captain, who had stopped eating and was holding the can of bread in front of him with his thumb and two moist fingers poised above it, clinging with gooey crumbs (the medic talking about the Army stockade at Long Binh, James—Long Binh Jail; LBJ, we called it). "I'd rather do hard time at LBJ," the man said, his voice suddenly loud and firm. "I ain't bullshittin' and I ain't crazy—and I ain't gonna medic for you no more!" The captain listened with great patience to the gulped whispers—holding that can of bread in front of himself— and did not argue, having looked into the medic's sickened face the whole time.

The captain said, "Fine. When the chopper comes you get on it and go back. Put your shirt on. Take your bag; take your ruck; leave the pistol," pointing to the .45 on the medic's hip—that .45 handed over from one company medic to the next for going on four years, James. For the sake of the paper-work the medic was reassigned as the permanent Phuc Luc Base Camp bunker-line aid-station medic—the all-night aid-station gofer and housecat—a job that didn't require a lick of work; the captain thinking to himself, Let's get *on* with this motherfucker.

The other, younger medic was called. The older medic un-strapped the .45 and gave it to the other man, swinging it off his hips by the buckle of the web belt and almost throwing it at the guy (classified two years before by his draft board as 1A-O—Conscientious Objector, but willing to serve—so they made him medic). Then the older medic dug deeply into his jacket pockets for the spare 8-round magazines; then taking the other medic's wrist he *put* those magazines of fresh rounds into his hand, as though he were settling a wager in that public and stubborn way that some men have.

"There. Treat 'em kindly. Just remember," the older medic said, "all's you're here for is to wrap them up, shoot them up, and shove them on a chopper. See ya." Then he scooped up his gear and walked to the chopper landing zone. The whole company stared at his back as they stood wiping the rain out of their eyes, choking down waterlogged rations, and getting ready for the inevitable morning move-out. The captain and all his men thought to themselves, There goes the company jinx, *now* maybe our luck will change!

Which it did, James, though not by much.

The medic mounted the chopper come to collect the body bags and the several tub-shaped thermoses as big as Coleman coolers (mermite cans, we called them) from the evening meal before. He sat slumped and resolute on the strap bench next to the portside-door gunner, with his rucksack and aid bag be-

tween his feet and his loaded rifle in his lap. The medic dismounted immediately when the chopper touched down at Phuc
Luc, as if he had been catapulted, throwing his beat-to-hell
rucksack over one shoulder and his aid bag over the other, like
a bum's bindles. He walked off the smooth, oily tarmac of the
chopper pad as though he had never seen that chopper before
in his life, and turned north up the hill toward the battalion
and the Bravo Company tents. He passed the base camp headquarters buildings, where the brigade staff lifers lounged in
the shade with their vodka-and-tonics in one hand and long
black cheroots in the other. He passed the base camp engineers
(Pacific Architects and Engineers, PA & E, we called them),
with their water-purification trucks and their portable cement
mixer, their concrete-block showers and walk-in ice locker. He
passed the spooky, deserted Alpha Company tents, now crawl-
ing with hordes of lawyers from the Judge Advocate General's
office, Red Cross do-gooders gathered from far and wide, and
freelance newspaper bird dogs (and that kind), scavenging,
pulling a nice fast buck for *Time* and *The Washington Post*
and *The Chicago Tribune*, and the rest. The headlines will
read:

F.B. HARRIETTE WIPED OUT

EXCLUSIVE PHOTOGRAPHS

SEC'TY VOWS MORE TROOPS

They stood around in small groups and gawked, scribbling
vigorous notes and names, snapping one another's picture and
pestering one another with questions and comments, mumbling asides. They rummaged through footlockers and duffel
bags and waterproof canvas bags, rifling through gear and pick-

ing at belongings that weren't any of their goddamned business, sucking on unlit pipes and shaking their heads at the pure and awful pity of it.

Finally the medic turned briskly up the Bravo Company street. The company clerks (typing their forms) and the mess cooks (stirring their Kool-Aid) and the housecat walking wounded (with their games of paper-scissors-stone) looked up, drawn to the sight of the medic, as if he were an apparition— "What on earth is the medic doing in camp," they said among themselves, "and why is the rest of the fucking company still in the field?" The medic turned sharply up the second path among the vacant company hooches to the left and disappeared into his own open-air hooch. He draped his rucksack and web gear and aid bag over the homemade headboard of his cot, peeled off his stinking jungle shirt, and went directly to the piss tube out back to relieve himself. Then, exhausted and sickly pale, he flopped headlong onto his cot, boots and all, and almost instantly fell asleep. He woke in the late afternoon, nearly nightfall, dripping with sweat, his face puffy and red with sleep and his mouth cotton dry; the quilted sleeping bag and poncho liner he used for a mattress well soaked.

By that time the word of his finding Paco and then quitting like that was all over camp. That night he sat in his hooch, with his feet up, eating leftover C-rations, smoking a whole mess of dope, listening to the loud and sticky keys of the company clerk's Underwood manual typewriter—tack-tack, tack-tack-tack-tack—the clerk writing home about that Alpha Company guy and the medic, all the while peeking at the medic through the screen door of the Orderly Room. For weeks and months afterward, until the medic rotated home in his proper turn, he stood on the ammunition-box stoop of his hooch (the company jinx), leaning on an ordinary push broom in the drooping canvas doorway, and watched the rest of Bravo Company come and go to the field—each time more scroungy and grungy and hangdog-looking than the time before. There were always fewer faces when they came humping those last three hundred meters up the hill from the base camp gate; always newer faces, pale and astonished, when they left camp again. Don't you know, a month or six weeks later, when the company came back through the gate and up that hill, those fucking new guys would be indistinguishable from the rest, except for the eyes. But the eyes took longer.

And ten, twelve, fifteen years later the medic will rock back and forth, night after night, in a chair near the wall of cases of bottled beer at the back of Weiss's Saloon, telling his stories. By the end of an evening (when it is good and dark) the medic will be good and drunk, but he can still crack those hard-boiled eggs and render the bleached shells neatly in two before he dips them in salt and then daubs each bite with hot mustard. And he's not so drunk he can't still drink his beers and shots right down (until one year soon he will simply drink himself sick, and die of it). Almost any night of the week he will sit there and brag that he could have made something of himself. "Would have been a goddamn *good* doctor, hear?" he will tell you, James, in his thick, alcoholic slur. "Except for this one guy, this *geek*," the guy not dead, but should have been.

3. The Thanks of a Grateful Nation.

Late in the crisp, sunny afternoon of an early spring day a silver-and-gray cross-country bus comes drifting up the quarter-mile exit ramp from the interstate toward an oversized STOP sign east of the town of Boone. Nearly everyone aboard squirms on their hams, rousing from a long afternoon of overpowering drowsiness. The driver—with a thin, clean face, well-manicured nails, and a tight paunch for a belly—downshifts with not so much as a lurch, while vigorously chewing a fresh stick of spearmint gum, cracking it sharply with a wide, hard grin. Near the top of the grade he downshifts again, coasting through the STOP sign, and turns onto the well-done two-lane state road. He wheels the bus, lumbering, onto the sun-warmed blacktop of the Texaco station where he often calls a ten-minute break. He eases the bus in a wide arc in front of the office and comes to a lilting halt. He cranks the emergency brake, turns the engine off, and lets go the air brakes with a loud, sweet whoosh.

Then the driver looks full in the mirror at the many faces

looking back at him, turns slightly in his seat, and says in a clear and mild voice, "This is the stop for Boone. There will be a ten-minute rest. All out for Boone." And the people begin struggling out of their seats, stiff and travel-weary. The driver pulls down his trip sheet, folded severely in thirds like a business letter, from the overhead visor and pencils in the arrival and departure times while glancing at the distinctive Swiss watch on his wrist (that watch, James, as fine as a chronometer). He files the crisply folded trip sheet, straightens up, and carefully unfolds and buttons his stiff shirt cuffs. And by the time he finishes and scans the seats again, only two people are left aboard, both still sleeping.

One is a frail old black woman slumped in a window seat near the front, who breathes deeply and sleeps soundly, hugging a dilapidated carpetbag crammed with odds and ends of knitting skeins, half-crocheted knickknacks, and a small polyethylene bag of warm plums. To see the other sleeper—our man Paco—the driver stretches and cranes his neck, leaning way out. Paco is curled sideways in his aisle seat, well toward the back, with his chin jammed into his shoulder, his hands wedged between his thighs, and his black hickory cane stuck between the seat cushions. He is not really asleep, hunched as awkwardly as he is, but mighty groggy from the several additional doses of medication—muscle relaxers and anti-depressants—to the point of a near-helpless stupor. His kidneys ache just like everyone else's, and he has a roaring, crushing headache. He often has these now. Paco is in constant motion, trying to get settled and comfortable with that nagging, warm tingling in his legs and hips. He is sore and cramped in a way that no amount of stretching and yawning, no exercises or therapies, can assuage. His whole body tingles and thrums with a glowing, suffocating uncomfortability that is more or less the permanent condition of his waking life.

But the driver, leaning out into the aisle and looking at Paco, doesn't know any of that. All he sees is some gimpy kid with a nice-looking cane. The driver pegged him for a GI when he got aboard (and you can always tell a GI homebound from overseas, James—underweight, funny eyes, dippy Army haircut), three-quarters stoned on some newfangled junk, no doubt. The driver grins and cracks his gum and shakes his head. He's been driving a bus for twenty-four years, and has seen it all: one-legged geeks fucking no-legged geeks on the long back seat; Colorado cowboys hauling bags of money aboard at Elko, Nevada, then hopping off, bags and all, before the bus gets halfway to Salt Lake and going back for more; bleary-eyed tourists boarding the wrong bus at Lafayette, then shrugging their shoulders and going where it was going; three old biddies from Georgia getting into a catfight about boyfriends; some old guy dying in his sleep coming into Duluth, stinking to high heaven when his bowels moved, and all those people wanting their money back. There'd been that pudgy little nymphomaniac who round-robined some semi-pro football team between Denver and Santa Fe; those identical twins with unmended harelips who could not make themselves understood no matter how hard they tried, "Smee, smoo-*smoo*, smish-smash," and the driver had belly-laughed all the way from Bakersfield to the Sacramento turnoff; that loony old bag from Watseka mumbling her mouth at him and anybody else who would listen, cackling and wheezing, "*Sonny-boy*, I well remember when this very motor coach would take you to the curb at the Walton Street entrance of the Drake Hotel"—Not in this life, the driver had thought to himself—"and this nice, clean, colored doorman would take your arm just so nice and polite when you stepped down, and he always wore a tall beaver hat, red velvet tails, and patent-leather shoes with dove-gray spats. So *handsome*, and just as clean as you please. My!" she said. There was the time those two goofy-looking hillbillies (bootie-busters for sure, the Memphis cop had said) went "flip" one afternoon, whipped out their skinning knives, and tried to hijack him and his bus to Duckbutter Ridge, or some such godawful place. He put both hands on the wheel, let them see the whites of his knuckles, and then told them to fold those goddamn knives *up* and sit *down*!—through clenched teeth— and was thoroughly surprised when they did. There'd been guys come aboard so ugly that you just knew God made them as ugly as He could, and then hit them with a stick; that big old fat woman, fattest woman he ever saw, who got all up in his shit because she'd paid her fare, she said—paid cash, she kept bragging—but could not for the life of her get through the doorway and up the coach steps, and as *sure* as hell wasn't going to fit into one of the seats. Goddamn, she was mad, and kept waving that little ticket of hers as though it were a hanky. There'd been wonder-struck Boy Scouts coming into New York for the first time over the George Washington Bridge ("Boy-oh-boy, will you look at all those lights!"); horny sailors bound for San Diego, prowling for pussy; New Orleans fags in Mardi Gras drag ("You, *Georgette*, are absolutely stunning," they had cooed and teased each other), stoned out of their fucking skulls on bennies and kef. There'd been Marines from Parris Island boot camp (Big deal, the driver had thought to himself), bound for Vietnam and falling-down shitfaced drunk on pints of Goon Squad vodka, who screamed marching songs and paro-dies of marching songs:

I don't know but I been told,
Eskimo pussy is mighty cold.
Know'd a woman dressed in black,
Made her living on her back.

Am I right or wrong?
You right!
Am I right or wrong?
You right!

I don't want to sit and cry!
I don't want to wonder why!
I just want to fight and die!

Am I right or wrong?
You right!
Am I right or wrong?
You right!

And they had spit marching commands in one another's faces: "Lef' 'ace, pussies. For'ard harch! An' ya'll better make me look good in front of the commandant or it'll be your assholes. Haw!" They had laughed and grinned, swilling that rotgut vodka and bouncing in their seats. "Warn't that honky somethin'?" And the driver had been flagged down at a grubby crossroad between Topeka and Salina, where some bald, muddy-eyed old geezer and his dumpy little hausfrau of a wife awkwardly hugged their kid. The kid, gaunt and bug-eyed, all neck and nose, leaving for the Navy (finally) and looking as though he's tolerating that preposterous deluge of affection for absolutely the last time; the little woman bawling her eyes out in a damp-dry dish-towel tucked into her apron; the old man right proud!—you could tell by the sparkle in his eyes.

The bus driver leans out into the aisle, looking back at Paco. He's seen GIs coming back plenty more shot up than this kid. Shit, take it all around, he ain't got it so bad—if this was Korea, 1953, he'd be pushing up daisies; if this was summer, 1945, he'd have been long gone. The driver walks back toward Paco, pulling himself along by the backs of the seats as though he's walking up an incline. "Hey, kid," he says clearly and firmly, cracking his gum a time or two. "Wake up. This is Boone. Far as you go, remember," he says, sniffing at the sharp scent of spearmint in his mustache and mindful of the distance between them. (The driver learned by vivid example years ago, James, to take care and keep an eye out when waking people up for their stop; he kept to the driving, and "As long as they don't leave a corpse behind," pretty much ignored the back of the bus.) The driver knows full well there is no one waiting for him in town, and he wants the thirty minutes it takes to get there and back for his own dinner.

"Wake up, kid," he repeats, more sharply. "End of the line."

Paco sleeps on, with his eyes squinted fiercely shut.

"Come on, troop. Last stop," the driver says, rocking on his hips, stretching, carefully exaggerating each word. "Off your ass and on your feet. Let's hit the silk." And Paco stirs, hearing this last.

"*That's* right. End of the line. Let's haul ass," the driver says.

And Paco moves with such a sudden jerk, such a startle, the driver spooks (he wouldn't be surprised if Paco lunged at him—they've done worse, these punks) and steps back quickly with a skip, giving Paco plenty of room to rise and stretch, and collect his gear. A moment later Paco stands on the bottom of the coach steps with his AWOL bag in one hand and his black hickory cane in the other, at the edge of a broad panorama of farmland and woods, greening up, with the warmth of the lowering sun full in his face, the shadows elongated. The bright spring sky is beginning to cloud over, and a clean, moist rain smell fills the air.

That frail old black woman, feigning sleep (dreamily luxuriating in the fragrance of those warm plums), watches Paco and the bus driver through the wrinkled-up slits of her eyes.

And meanwhile, the driver right behind Paco—both he and Paco feel the heat of the sun on their faces, smell the coming rain, the lingering diesel exhaust, and, too, the odor of those warm plums—the driver shags him right along, saying, "Town's west of here. No sweat, kid. It's getting toward quitting time. Hang your thumb out and *some*body's bound to be passing through on their way to town, sure. All the good bars're in town." Paco, still groggy, takes him at his word and steps onto the blacktop, and walks awkwardly—cramps, bad legs, crammed-full AWOL bag, black hickory cane, and all— around the side of the building to the foul little men's room that reeks almost painfully of disinfectant.

Now, James, when the interstate bus would pull in, it was a chance for the mechanics to slack off work and take a break. They would lounge on the edge of the desk near the door in their greased-up overalls, drinking hot coffee from filthy plastic picnic mugs. In the coldest weather the boss would leave a pint of cheap whiskey in the drawer along with the stacks of skin magazines (*All-Star Tit Queens* and *Bikes, Black Leather, and Big Broads*).

The minute Paco is out of sight the driver goes into the station, pours himself a Styrofoam cup of thick, well-boiled coffee, and chats with the two mechanics—Chuck and Duck—giving them his regards, then discreetly gathers his passengers into the bus with the quiet suggestion that time is nearly up. The driver starts the bus, waiting for the air pressure to come up to snuff; everyone boards for the last bit of traveling before dinner. Meanwhile, Paco is stripped to the waist and dousing himself with handful after handful of cold water, gritting his teeth and catching his breath. Then he dries his hands and face and under his arms with handfuls of damp, limp paper towels the texture of newsprint, smears his chest with dime-store aftershave, puts on a clean shirt puckered with wrinkles and a windbreaker got secondhand in a Salvation Army thrift store. The driver watches for Paco in the outside rearview mirror, and when he emerges around the side of the building, the driver slips the bus into gear and rolls off, saying out loud that the next stop will be the dinner hour. The bus swings out onto the two-lane; Paco crosses the blacktop parkway, the heat rising into his plain low-quarter oxfords. The driver steers cleanly with one hand, reaching into this bag underneath the seat for his Bausch & Lomb aviators; Paco stands over his crammed-full AWOL bag on the broad gravel shoulder. He leans on his cane with both hands, sits down, and watches for oncoming traffic through the blue-black exhaust fumes and sparkling road dust up-swirled behind the bus. The driver adjusts his aviators and glances down at the outside rearview, seeing Paco again, squatted on that tight-packed bag of his, and the driver pulls onto the entrance ramp of the interstate with slow-motion eagerness. Then the old black woman—who's been snuggling up to her carpetbag, napping and daydreaming all afternoon—suddenly opens her eyes. She sees Paco for only an instant (still mindful of the scene between the driver and Paco not five minutes before), his cane as thin as a pencil and his eyes the points of pins, and instantly, vividly remembers her own son come home from the Korean War in nineteen and fifty-three, standing in the doorway of their old shotgun house in those baggy, travel-dirty khakis of his; who said not a word about the war; who was ever after morose and skittish, what folks round about miscalled lazy and no-'count; who had ever since lapsed into a deep and permanent melancholy. Paco stares hard at the bus, broadside (seeing the whites of the old woman's tiny eyes), until it slides down the ramp and is gone —thinking, This sure ain't the first fucking time I've been left behind; thinking what any grunt would think to himself, Whatever happens after, Jack, whatever comes next (and I just about give a sweet fuck, you understand), let's just get a fucking move on and get to it.

When the bus pulls away the two mechanics knock back the dregs of their coffee, getting motivated, as the boss would say, and move back toward their work. All this time one mechanic (Chuck, it is) has been shaking his hand and fingers, and grinning painfully for all to see, trying to work the sting out of his knuckles where he jammed them on the transmission of the Chevy jacked up on the far hoist—the meat of his knuckles burning with solvent. He looks out the window (streaked with filth) at Paco sitting astride his AWOL bag, distractedly digging the brass tip of his cane into the loose gravel between his feet. The young mechanic sees the hickory cane and thinks, What would possess a guy with such a stiff limp to hitch? Well, we get all kinds, and I guess it takes all kinds. He pours himself another cup of coffee and sits back down on the edge of the greasy desk, swinging his leg, and says, drawling, "Hey, Duck! Why don't we crank up old Rupert and give that guy a lift to town"—Rupert, the station's flashy, customized GMC tow truck bristling with three or four kinds of antennae, and many white and amber Mars lights—"Maybe I'll stop at the clinic and have Mildred do up my hand!" he says, and flicks his bad hand a time or two more.

The other mechanic, older by a couple of years—a thick little guy with his overalls unbuttoned to the crotch—noisily rifles through a high tool cabinet. He pauses when he comes to the timing light. "Naw!"—out on the roadway Paco stretches his back, yawning—"Naw! Let 'im walk. You just want some fucking excuse to go to town and piss around at Rita's. You looking for something to do, park that goddamned Chevy and pull in that green Olds and dismount the snow tires. Radials are in the trunk. And hustle it up, the boss says the guy's coming for it by six."

Hearing that, the young mechanic tosses his plastic picnic mug, coffee and all, into an old oil drum piled with the detritus that accumulates around any good gas station near any well-traveled interstate. He charges out the door, making for the Olds. But the more he works his hand, grimacing with a fine theatrical air, the more his curiosity gets the best of him, so he winds up circling the Olds and climbing into the tow truck—the name Rupert printed backward on the front hood, so you can read it in your rearview. The truck is decked out with one of those waxy-looking, titsy little Kewpie-doll air fresheners hanging from the inside mirror, a gun rack across the back window, Naugahyde seatcovers, an acrylic necker's knob on the steering wheel, a full set of heavy-duty oversized snow tires, mud flaps as big as doormats (studded with many purple reflectors), a Teflon-coated slant-blade snowplow and fancy running boards; the whole contraption painted maroon and orange like the Milwaukee Road's *Hiawatha*—just dripping with silver-and-black curlicued pinstriping and sparkling with chrome trim. At night, under the station's many huge, fluorescent lamps, that truck would shimmer like a Christmas tree in warm light.

The young mechanic cranks it up—rapping the straight pipes that curl behind the cab, the crackle of the pipes shaking the station windows—and rolls easy-like out to the highway and gives Paco a ride to town. The older mechanic comes out the big bay doorway, holding that timing light like a toy pistol, and yells, "You come right back, hear? You come right back! We got work! Have Mildred fix your fucking hand and *you come right back! You hear?*" Then he mutters, "Goddamn that lazy son-of-a-bitch!"

The young mechanic drives easy, mindful of his speed and gears, certainly not in a hurry on such a fine spring day. And, of course, to pass the time he and Paco talk, the kid steering with the necker's knob and asking questions, and Paco sitting awkwardly forward—grateful for the ride, you understand—with his AWOL bag between his feet, keeping an eye out for town and answering politely. "Where you from? Where you bound? Why the cane? Was the fighting as bad as they say? Well, I got bad feet—had bad feet all my life—otherwise, you bet, I'da damn joined, you can bet!" Paco tells the kid he didn't miss a goddamned thing, says the kid should count himself lucky. And after a mile or so the conversation finally thins out to an awkward silence, but the kid, eager to palaver, finally asks, "What happened after they took you out of that place?"—after Paco mentioned the holocaust massacre at Fire Base Harriette.

Paco sits forward even more on the warm seat, afraid to lean back and relax, because the medication makes him drowsy and stupid and he doesn't want to fall asleep. He holds his cane in both hands, turning it round and round. "Nothing much, I guess," he says, and glances over at the kid driving with one hand on the necker's knob and the other hand slapping the hollow of the door in 4/4 time—the kid's bloody knuckles shining, numb with the cold.

"They had me so zonked out on morphine I don't much remember," Paco says, "you know?" and that closes the subject.

But Paco remembers all right, and vividly.

There was the big red cross on the white field on the bottom of the medevac chopper when it came to get him, and nearly the instant he was aboard the chopper rose with a swoop, making speed and altitude swiftly. Paco's stomach fluttered and he felt mighty dizzy, and he thought he was going to throw up. He remembers the healthy, browned faces of the medics, and their gossip about the filthy debris in Paco's wounds—the maggots in the running sores (almost the feeling of an enticing caress), the soft, spongy scabs on burst blisters, and the crusts of dirt. He remembers the peculiar sensation (this through several quarter-grain doses of morphine) when the boldest of the medics—an earnest-looking guy with a firm, light touch and cool fingers—started picking at strips of cloth and splinters of wood, bits of blackened, brittle skin as long and curled as razor-clam shells (the pink, raw skin burning)—the medics thinking it was like picking chips of old paint from a thick coat of new paint, still tacky. All the while, the other medics soothed Paco, petting him, saying, "Gonna be okay, hey! You gonna be cool in another ten minutes. Okay! Can't fuck up a tough motherfucker like you, now can they?" And they kept saying okay to him, as though it was part of their work. And they'd ask him, "Who *are* you, Jack? What's your *name*? What *happened* there?" shouting over the whining, rushing engine noises. And all that time Paco kept one thought in his head as distinct as a colorful dream—I must not die—each word reverberating as though said out loud, the crisp pronunciation tingling the sore flesh of his mouth—*I must not die*—like the litany of an invocation, as though he felt his body shrink each instant he did not say it. And he remembers being overwhelmed with tears (though half the medics expected a wan, plucky smile), his swollen mouth watering and his eyes and nose burning with tears, again and again—because he *was* alive; because he had made it (thanks to God's luck, James)—the moisture cold on his face in the brisk rotor wash of the chopper blades. He remembers flying at a solid thousand feet, making a beeline for the western perimeter at Phuc Luc (so they could turn straight to the hospital dust-off pad without having to circle above the wards to come into the wind)—the young chopper pilot turning his head now and again, asking how the wounded guy was, and the medics telling him, "Just keep hauling ass, Jack!" And the pilot swerved this way and that among the huge monsoon thunderheads to avoid their fierce weather, flying full-bore flat-out, James, just as fast as that machine would fly.

Paco stretched his neck and looked out the wide chopper doorway, and it was noon, remember, and there before him

was a brilliant panorama of thunderheads in every direction—
fleece-white and gunmetal-gray, and black as thick as night.
They rose thousands of feet into the air, billowing up majesti-
cally, the same as Spanish dancers rising out of a deep curtsy,
sweeping open their arms (an overpowering image of God's
power shown to us in a small way, James). The slow-motion
billows towered up and up above Paco and the others; some
sailed serenely on; others rained hard, pounding downpours of
monsoon storms, soaking the ground to mush. All the many
storms drifted like sleepwalkers climbing a broad balcony stairway, Paco thought as he looked out the chopper—the lilting
rain cascaded down like the lacy trains of airy ballgowns,
trailing behind the dreamlike sleepers. And then it seemed to
him that the thunderheads looked like plain, stern young
women with long, loosened hair, standing here and there and
yonder on a smooth stone quay, waiting for a dream death
ship, say; each woman with her small clean hands folded
lightly across a hard, swollen belly; each standing well away
from the others, while pigeons pecked about underfoot, swarm-
ing for crumbs, and a hot, breathtaking sun beat down over all.

Well below the chopper the jungle looked spongy soft, as
though Paco could have reached down into it—like reaching
into the rich suds of a green bubble bath—and scooped up a
frothy handful; Paco was sure it would be the most fragrant
foam. Here and there the brilliant sunlight caught patches of
water—rice paddies and irrigation ditches, ordinary hooch-
yard puddles and snatches of some river or other through the
jungle canopy, and bomb craters as big as house lots—the
reflections caught his eye like a fierce light through the chinks
in a wood fence, more stunning and fantastic than muzzle
flashes. Paco saw the broad swaths of water-filled craters, the

truck convoys making headway among the woods and curves and storms—dust rising above the dry sections of roadway—the old tank laagers where the tank treads had dug furrows in the thick, squishy turf.

Paco and the medics floated through that bizarre, horrific gloom in the broad light of day, with the air smelling of damp electricity. The rain slanted one way (the spray sucked into the rotor wash), indistinct and misted; the scorching midday sun slanted another, the colors and shadows crisp and vivid, as radiant and sharp as a bright and interesting face seen in a clean mirror.

The dust-off flew, pounding, over the perimeter at Phuc Luc above the sweltering bunker line bristling with guns, then banked downwind, eastward, making for the sandbagged hospital compound (you could see the huge red crosses on the many compound rooftops)—the air in the chopper suddenly hot and bright above the bare ground and tin roofs. Nearly everyone in the chopper's path looked up from his work to watch it cruise overhead—every man understanding full well that the one survivor of the Alpha Company holocaust massacre was aboard, half wrapped in a body bag and still alive (Can you beat that!), otherwise the pilot would not still be flying so hard. The chopper came swiftly, steeply in, making directly for that bit of tarmac at the end of the duckboard walkway outside the awning of the hospital triage. It settled quickly and firmly on the chopper pad. The triage medics, the zonked-out Graves Registration slick-sleeve privates, and other passersby and hangers-on hustled out to help—to gawk, too, no doubt; to touch luck, we might think, James—and brought Paco into the stuffy shade of the triage tent and laid him on one of those waist-high litter racks for the duty officer to inspect—everyone talking at once, taking pictures.

A triage is the place in the back of a hospital where the litter bearers line up the wounded brought in from the field; first come first served, you understand. A doctor examines them, culling through the wounds, comparing and considering, then picks who's first in the operating room, who's second, who's last—and who gets written off. In extreme emergencies the worst hopeless cases are drugged, usually with healthy doses of morphine, shunted off to the Moribund Ward, and allowed to die among themselves with only one another for comfort. And once you are taken into the Moribund Ward, James, you are as good as dead—no matter how long it takes. But Paco, by then famous as the nameless wounded man from Alpha Company's massacre, got every consideration.

The doctor, a pasty-faced major with a fresh pair of operating greens bloused sloppily into his jungle boots, swaggered into the open-air triage, wiping his hands on a mildly bloody apron like a fishmonger's wife. He took one look at Paco and saw immediately that he was unfit to take into the operating room. He knew also that they would be swamped with equally serious wounded, and plenty of them, from the bloodbath firefight at Fire Base Francesca as soon as a chopper could make it through the withering ground fire and RPGs, and that they—the doctors and nurses and medics—might well work through the night. Indeed, James, that was pretty much what happened. The doctor unzipped Paco's body bag—the sharp raw stench of Paco's wounds, Paco's bowels, rising fully in his face. He turned the bloody zippered flaps of the bag this way and that, reaching in to lift a scrap of cloth to inspect the festering wounds and the bone fragments that stuck through the skin. "Christ Jesus on a bloody fuckin' crutch," he said under his breath, "how long was this guy left like this?— what's his name?"

"Almost two days," said the medic with the good hands. "This is that Alpha Company guy and he ain't said who he is yet, sir."

(It must have been one motherfucker of a firefight, the medics and nurses said among themselves as they looked on, and ended the night steeped in blood.)

The major looked over at Paco again and said, "Right." And then, because Paco was stinking filthy and peppered with minute flakes and slivers of shrapnel, he said, "Take this man into a side room here and scrub him up," dropped the flaps of the body bag, and wiped his hands on his apron—his nose smarting the same as everyone else's—"Then we'll take a look at him and start to work." So the triage medics shot Paco another quarter-grain of morphine, grabbed a couple bottles of Phisohex surgical soap and a handful of scrub brushes, jerked him and his litter up, and hustled him into a side cubicle.

Paco remembers the stiff, greasy canvas drapes the medics pulled to, the hot light bulb with the jerry-rigged wires hanging in his face, the medics pouring sweat, the collapsed garbage bag of rotted field dressings in the corner—that oppressive and fetid, suffocating air. He remembers, too, oddly, the sweet and medicinal smell of the soap, and the sloppy, squishy sound of the lather.

Paco was warm and numb from the morphine (as though tucked up snugly in stiff, thick blankets) when they smeared the first doses of surgical soap on his chest and arms, then commenced to scrub him raw. When the shot finally took full effect, Paco felt only a vague grinding sensation, that was all, as though someone were gouging the stringy meat and seeds from a ripe pumpkin with a blunt wooden spoon; it sounded as though they were scrubbing coarse cloth, bearing down with great vigor. He remembers lolling his head back on the small, flat pillow (a burlap sandbag stuffed with loose dressings), and finally, the welcome ease of sleep that came over him after nearly two days of his earnest and stoic, watchful anticipation of death. (It was something the same as the first moment you slipped off your 60–80–100-pound rucksack pack—that instantly dumb, numb, inexpressible relief when your shoulders, your lungs, your kidneys seemed to float upward, and your whole torso tingled and throbbed, ached and itched—like a foot and leg asleep. It felt like a hard task finally ended; not done well, mind you, James, simply done with.)

Now scrubbing out the shrapnel with Phisohex and surgical scrub brushes was a common first-aid procedure—comfort of the wounded had nothing to do with it, and most never got the consideration of morphine, "Waste of good dope, Jack!"—more common certainly than having some first-of-May, fucking-new-guy rookie triage medic sit there picking at a million slivers of shrapnel with a manicure scissors, a magnifying glass, and a bottle of hydrogen peroxide. So the medics, wearing surgical masks and gagging at the stench, peeled back the black rubber body bag bit by bit and cut off the remains of Paco's clothes with surgical scissors as they went about the business of cleaning him up for his first surgery.

Paco awoke in what must have been the middle of the night in the stifling heat of a squalid little Quonset hut, the Recovery Ward, coming out of the anesthetic with his legs and back itchy and prickly, feeling as though someone were chop-

ping into them with a tailor's scissors as big as a shears—
skrit, skrit, skrit (the bosomy night nurse sitting at the nurses'
station scribbling notes on charts with a bit of pencil in a
small circle of harsh light)—Paco thinking that when an arm
or leg is amputated you often have the sensation, later, that
the amputated part itches or feels hot or cold. He felt the bed-
sheets tighten and slacken against his chest; felt his own
breathing. He heard the bugs banging on the coppery screen
of the door under the porch light, the hiss coming in over a
radio receiver somewhere (white noise, we called it), someone
walking on the duckboard outside, the duckboard slapping into
shallow puddles. All of that immediate and simultaneous with
someone's endless moaning, rhythmic and sustained—another
of the wounded men in the ward letting go, breath by breath,
of some deep and woeful hurt. Paco opened his eyes with a
blink and whispered, "Hey," just to hear the sound of his own
voice—the same as you might pinch yourself, James, to prove
that you are substance, and awake and alive, after all. And
the bosomy night nurse snapped her head around and looked
across the way, quickly searching a roomful of vigorously
healthy bodies suddenly extremely ill (instant amputations
and cracked skulls, shredded organs and disembowelments,
faces destroyed by close-in AK rifle fire—the slugs still em-
bedded in the heads—the smell of heavy, foul sweat); the
many IV bottles and the many drooping amber tubes; a huge
pedestal fan whirring like crazy in the corner; the stainless-
steel trays arranged just so in the nightstands; and the sparkles
of light arching across the curved Quonset ceiling. The instant
the woman turned her attention to the room, everything was
chugging and ticking, hissing and thunking, rasping shrilly,
and the men were jerking and gasping, but sleeping hard. They

52

were so whacked out on painkillers they could not see and could not feel and could not smell anything except the sickly, rank medicinal odor of the bandages and the bloody slop of their own body rot, scabbing over—everything seemed a million miles below them, behind them, around back of them or up on the eight hundredth shelf and unfathomly, unreachably beyond them; as good as echoes. One man gritted his teeth and grimaced, rolling his eyes. Another man stretched and curled his toes, wrinkled his brow, squinched and blinked his eyes, as though he were counting the freight cars of a passing train. Another man pumped his legs as if he were pedaling a bike, and squirmed as though his bed were spread with rock salt, steam puffing out the holes in his oxygen mask in quick steady chugs. The night nurse saw Paco stretching and rustling around, pulling at the sheets gathered in his fists, trying to glimpse the end of his bed where his legs were, plastered and bandaged, as thick as bedposts. She dropped her paperwork and went immediately to him and sat lightly on the very edge of his bed. At first she reassured him, telling him where he was: "The post-op ward of the evac hospital, and you've had an operation, and you'll have more, but you're okay," she said, and gave him a drink of tepid water, holding the tall Styrofoam cup steady while he sipped deeply through the plastic straw; Paco always especially remembered her rich, feminine voice. "What is your name?" she said. "Tell me your name, say your name." So he told her, though he discovered he could barely speak, and in that same instant he tried to take hold of her jungle trousers with the very tips of his fingers—his hands deeply cut, bruised, burned, heavily bandaged. He wanted to ask her who all these men were; if there was *anyone* from Alpha Company, *anyone* else from Fire Base Harriette? "No," she said clearly, anticipating him, "these are from Fire Base Francesca. You're the *only* one from Harriette." And Paco eased back on the bed, lapsing into thought about that, absorbing it. She gave him another shot of morphine—the surgeon had left orders to give him plenty, but not *too* much, because if the kid croaked he'd hear about it from every son-of-a-bitch in the chain of command and his career would be up shit creek. Then the woman pulled the sheet back (the smell of clean meat there)—Paco remembered always the smell of her Ivory soap and her face shining in the low light, and how her blouse clung to her body as she moved. She peeled back the stiff bandages (Paco mesmerized by the crackle of them, so many bandages) and then gave him a sponge bath with a soft hand towel rinsed in a shallow basin of water fetched from the ward's water cooler. The nurse went about her work with that calm and soothing patience some women have who understand full well the need for physical kindness and its effect—a fondness for the warm touch of care that is just as often a caress—she daubing his body clean bit by bit with a cool cloth and warm hands. Soon after she commenced, Paco got an erection (not as uncommon as you might think, James; after all, we'd been in the field for nearly forty-five days and Paco hadn't been with a woman for months before that). The nurse washed Paco's belly and watched his cock stand fully erect (a dozen or so knotted stitches pinching; Paco mightily embarrassed— the woman a nurse, a stranger after all, an officer, for Christ's sake!), but she discouraged the hard-on with a half-dozen hard flicks of her fingernail—the same as she would tap the morphine syringe to get rid of air bubbles, only harder. She washed his face and ears, combing back his hair with her hands and fingers. She redressed his wounds, pulled the sheet back to his chin, and soon he was fast asleep. Later that morning, before breakfast, the major (looking plainly exhausted) made the rounds of the wards—coming along first thing, in clean operating greens, to check on Paco and the other dozen wounded. The blousy night nurse stood with a hand on Paco's bed rail and casually mentioned that she thought the guy from the Alpha Company massacre would make it fine (none of the hospital staff ever did call him by his name). And bit by bit, day by day, he did get better, though he shit blackish, pasty stool for weeks.

Some smart-ass put the snips of shrapnel (hard metal shavings the color of coconut flakes), the misshapen rifle slugs, the sharply jagged pieces of brass shell casings, the pieces of bones which they couldn't fit—all that—into a petri dish and slipped it in with Paco's other meager belongings (fetched from his gear at Alpha Company) stashed under the nightstand. And weeks later, when Paco first saw the dish while he was sorting through his gear, it reminded him of those chintzy little souvenir saucers filled with pins and buttons and other trivial oddments that folks keep out of sheer senti-mentality. Paco kept that petri dish, of course.

The night nurse tended him carefully, talking with him, protecting him from the Red Cross do-gooders and the brigade chaplain. She watched him sleep from her chair at the nurses' station across the room, bathed him every night with that same soft cloth and warm efficiency. Then one night while she bathed him, not long after he arrived, she wiped her hands of soap and encouraged an erection. His cock, dotted with stitch-ing, rose from between his thighs with quick jerks—a fine, firm hard-on, though all he felt through the dazzling morphine was a peculiar fullness. The woman took hold of it with one hand and, caressing his belly with the other, leaned down and licked the head (shining like an oiled plum) with her swirling tongue, and gingerly caressed it more and more with her warm fingertips (the stitches stretching, stinging). He put his hands on her head and worked his fingers into her short hair—astonished, luxuriating in the wonderful pleasure (a sweet, toothache pain). A good long time she masturbated him, sucking languorously, and soon enough he felt the pause and urge of terrific inevitability. She sensed it, too (the muscles of his buttocks hunching under the bandages), reached for a large bandage, and clapped it over the head of his cock. And when he climaxed he went on and on. She cleaned him up, dusted his crotch with talc, and Paco felt fine, considering the stitches—just fine.

Then one night Paco was softly, abruptly awakened by two strapping medics, doped with an unscheduled shot of morphine, laid on a litter from the triage, loaded on a regular Huey chopper waiting at the dust-off pad with its running lights blinking, and brought—plaster casts, IV bottles, tubes, and all—to Tan Son Nhut Air Base on the outskirts of Saigon. Paco and several other deathly wounded, plus a couple of guys they waited better than two hours for, were strapped to tiered racks in the dim, reddish light of the spartan cargo bay, given another healthy dose of morphine, and flown to hospitals in Japan where they could get better treatment, prosthetics and skin grafts, and whatnot; where they could convalesce in heightened comfort and superb peace. During the flight, metal cabinets slammed open and shut, and the plane jerked and swung and vibrated like a thousand needles. Paco lay on his litter in the rack with his arms squeezed against his sides, holding clenched fists over his groin. He gritted his teeth, rolled his head back and forth to assuage the pain, and endured it as best he could (along with the other wounded) in gripping silence. Travel time was every minute of five solid hours. Two of the several wounded brought in from the bitter fighting around Ban Me Thuot bled to death, whimpering, because the medics could not staunch their wounds, which soaked through everything—field dressings and hospital dressings, skimpy blankets and litter canvas—the blood glistening.

One evening at the hospital in Japan a pasty-faced full-bird colonel from Westmoreland's MACV headquarters in Saigon arrived in Paco's room with a retinue of curious staff doctors and well-behaved nurses to give Paco his medals—a Purple Heart and a Bronze Star. The colonel wore a fat wedding ring, his sleeves crisply folded above the crook of his elbow, and jungle trousers tailored nicely and bloused neatly into his immaculately spit-shined jungle boots. Paco was still wrapped in bandages head to toe, his legs and hips packed in solid plaster casts. The colonel leaned over the head of the bed—the doctors horning in to clear away some of the bandages around Paco's head right and proper—and a keen startled look came into his eyes as the doctors unraveled more and more dressings and the colonel encountered Paco's wounds. Suddenly awkward, he opened his musette bag and laid the medal cases on the night table. He pinched some of the material of Paco's hospital pajamas together above the breast pocket, slipped the pin of the Purple Heart through, and clasped it. His clean, well-manicured hands smelled of expensive, woodsy pipe tobacco. "For wounds suffered," he said in a low and steady voice, whispering just loud enough for everyone in the room to hear. Then he took up the Bronze Star. "For particular bravery," he said, repeating a key phrase in the citation, pinning the medal crooked and close to the other so that there was a mumbling buzz of comment in the softly lit room because the medals were draped oddly across his bandages. The colonel leaned over even farther, pressing Paco into the mattress somewhat, and whispered something in his ear. And Paco can never remember what it was the man said, as many times as he has puzzled over it, but *always* recalls the warm breath on the side of his head and in his hair. (Paco had the distinct memory *then* of when he was a small boy and his father would come into his darkened bedroom some evenings, in his rawhide slippers and baggy pants, sit down lightly on the edge of his bed, and sing him to sleep in that whispering, croaking voice of his:

> *Here comes the sandman,*
> *Stepping so softly,*
> *Stealing around on the tips of his toes,*
> *As he scatters the sand with his sure little hand,*
> *In the eyes of sleepy children.*

Paco remembered the warm, firm caresses of his father rubbing his back, and how the song always provoked yawns, and how his father would lean down and kiss his face when he had finished.)

The colonel fumbled with the ribbons and the cases and the tissue-paper citations, a sheen of tears welling in the man's eyes as he straightened up and left the room, saying to Paco, "Goodbye, young sergeant," with the doctors and nurses right behind.

That was the reason Paco never threw away the medals, or pawned them, as many times as he was tempted and as stone total worthless as the medals were—the Army gave them out like popcorn, you understand, like rain checks at a ball park. It is the kiss he cherishes and the memory of the whispered word. He has the medals still, packed in the shaving kit of his AWOL bag under the seat of that done-up tow truck from the Texaco station—the medal cases smeared with shaving soap and soaked with dimestore aftershave, and the citations folded up as small as matchbooks.

4. Paco Coming into Town.

The mechanic wheels that tow truck up the two-lane state road toward the outskirts of town, past smart, well-built bungalows and neat, tight little trailer homes. He turns onto the broad pea-gravel parking lot of Rita's Tender Tap, with a clatter of tow chains and pry bars and other hefty tools loose in the back of the truck, just short of the town's river bridge.

Now, Rita's looks like many another roadhouse bar in this broad world—driveway gutted with chuckholes, dwarfed spruce across the front, large tinted windows framing neon beer signs that buzz and crackle, and a big decal on the glass of the front door—a skinny little runt with a dufus, toothy grin, a nose like a thimble, bulging contrary eyes, apple cheeks, and plenty of acne, holding up scrolled parchment that's curled at the top and bottom (like a proclamation, James) and reads:

NO SHIRT

NO SHOES

NO SERVICE

Underneath someone had written in:

NO BOY SCOUTS

And someone had written in under that:

NO SHIT

Around the building are parked Oldses and Mercs, Buicks and Caddies (all settled low on their rear springs), rusted-out Chevies, banged-up pickups spattered with pasture muck, panel trucks and step-in vans, and last but not least a couple of Wyandotte County road-crew dump trucks with the salt spreaders still mounted on back.

Chuck, the mechanic, parks the truck. Paco takes his AWOL bag and thanks him for the lift this far, and starts making his way to the bridge. But the mechanic, not having the sense to know when enough is enough, insists that Paco accept the offer of a beer, saying, "Come on, *boy*, I just done you a good turn. Come on," while pulling at Paco's arm.

Just then it begins to rain, so Paco submits to the hospitality and they go into Rita's together.

You can always tell the clientele by the look of what's parked in the lot. Salesmen drumming Snap-On tools and CBs, Bibles and other inspirational literature (*Find God, End the Horrible Misery in Your Life, Be Free with Jesus!*); drinking neat whiskey. Absolute stone-total losers and day-labor ne'er-do-wells on their way to California or Nevada or Oregon or Alaska to try what's left of their luck out there; drinking Rita's cheapest American beer. Guys blowing their VFW poker-night winnings on a trip to Florida to look over some dirt-cheap "investment" property; drinking Jack Daniel's and water. Small-time speculators who look at the countryside around them and see nothing but riches or lean times —let's turn a nickel's profit, Jack, then skedaddle; drinking bar Scotch-on-the-rocks. And, *too*, there are those two truckloads of Wyandotte County maintenance-department rednecks, loafing in grand style, who always spend the last hour of their shift at Rita's before they hustle over to the garage and clock out. The road crews belly up to the bar, swilling mugs of Pabst Blue Ribbon on tap, or bottles of Hamm's, flashing their pinkie rings, sporting those snappy-looking rough-rider high-top work boots with the fancy mountaineer laces, and those sleeveless work vests (camouflage-colored on one side and Day-Glo orange on the other). And they carry pouches and plugs of Day's Work and Red Man and Mail Pouch tobacco, and tins of scented snuff. All of them wear those baseball-style caps— brand-new items with the De Kalb Coop logo, with a grinning Poland-China pig or leghorn rooster or a flying yellow corncob.

Everyone in the place drinks his beer and such, nibbling warmed-over popcorn and Beer Nuts and Slim Jims, and flirts with Rita, a tall, healthy-looking woman with a large head of hair, a pink-and-black bartender's outfit, and a "nice set of big ones," the rednecks will tell you, James. Rita knows how to flirt with the best of them, throwing her head back and slapping the flat of her chest and laughing out loud, saying, "Oh, you George Luntke! Oh, Georgie, you're such a damn tease! Such a damn card!

> *Georgie Porgie, puddin' 'n' pie,*
> *Kissed the gals and made them cry . . ."*

She'd rhyme and chime, "Why, you just would, too, you old fart." Rita would trade jibes with anyone, the regulars and the passersby. She knows how to hustle her tips, cadging watered-down drinks or buying the bar a round on someone's birthday (or some manufactured occasion), to prime the drinkers.

An overhead light shines through the rack of glassware above Rita's head, and it dazzles everything in the place— liquor spills, wristwatches, clean hair, rings and charms and flashy bracelets, pens in pockets, lacquered nail polish, the crisp sheen of starched collars, and all the wood trim round and about. The rednecks, sitting together at the far end of the bar, playing dice games for drinks, quickly welcome Chuck and acknowledge Paco with blunt stares. They immediately cross-examine Chuck about Duck, the other mechanic. They razz him about the big deal he wants to make about a couple skinned knuckles when Chuck shows his hand to Rita for some mother's sympathy and a bit of meaningless first aid.

"Po' little Chuckie," one of the rednecks (in a gray-and-green flannel shirt) croons and pines. "Hurt his little hand an' fingers. Cain't get no poontang wid a ugly Ban'Aid on yo han'," the guy swoons around, hanging on to the bar, eyeballing the rest of the rednecks. "Why the poon take one good look at that in the broad light of the day an' say, 'Oh, Chuckie-wuckie, dat's so nasty! Behave now an' put dat back in yo pocket, wike a good widdle boy. Ah'd love to roll in da hay wit-cha, my sweetes' little patootie, but ah got the rag awn dis ev'nin', puddin'. Y'all call me when yo healed up some, eh?'" And the guy in the flannel shirt slaps the bar and reels around on his stool, scooping up the dice and knocking back his beer, while everyone else laughs and laughs. Even Chuck laughs, accustomed to being the butt of their jokes and pranks.

Just like a fucking new guy, Paco thinks to himself as he slides a leg over a stool and hangs the handle of his cane on the bar. Let's have our beer, and drink our beer, and when the rain lets up, we'll move on.

One guy at the middle section of the bar grins at the game and tosses some loose bar change along the bar among the glasses and napkins and liquor spills, and offers to buy the kid a shot of "real whiskey, to put some guts into him," when they operate to fix the kid's hand, once and for all. Rita taps the beers for Paco and the young mechanic, then goes to the back to fetch the first-aid kit. Another of the rednecks, a guy with an Adam's apple that sticks out like an elbow, says, "Well, shit, Chuckie m'boy, who's yer friend?" in a tone both polite and menacing, indicating Paco with a crisp nod.

Paco rubs the sweating mug of beer with the pad of his thumb. "My name's Paco. Just arrived on the bus. Looking for work; know any? Looking for a place to stay." And that is all he says, thinking, Answer straight, talk in a normal tone of voice, drink the beer, and leave as soon as the rain lets up.

The kid with the Adam's apple leans over the bar and into the light, and says, "Well, shit, fella, you might as well keep fuckin' beatin' feet, as they say. Ain't that what they say?"

"You're telling me there ain't no work?" says Paco.

64

"Ain't no work around this neck of the woods but good, is what I'm saying. Ain't that right?" he says, and looks around at the rest of the rednecks on his crew. "Sure as shit. Fuckin'-A. Fuckin' foundry mill's gonna close any day now. Railroad, which used to hire any goddamned gimpy deadbeat that come up the pike"—the guy has seen Paco's cane, just like everyone else in the place—"even they gettin' picky and pissy and don't hardly hire *no*body no more. Fuckin' Fisher-body up at Griffin's been laying off motherfuckers left and right every pay period." (All this sterling advice, James, from a kid who has been on the dole—one way or another—all his life, and even owes his county job to his uncle. The kid will shovel sand and road salt and cold-patch asphalt off the back of a dump truck with a long-handled ditch spade for thirty years—at the prevailing wage, you understand. And if he behaves himself, and his uncle's cronies approve, one fine day they'll give him a Pay-loader or backhoe or even a road grader—at the prevailing wage. And he'll retire slick and clean, with a belly as solid as a nail keg, but seldom in all those years will he ever crank a decent day's work.)

"My ad-vice," the guy says, putting a big pinch of pepper-mint snuff back of his lip, "is that you hustle your ass back on out to the Texaco and catch yourself another bus on out of here, and take it just as far as your money will get you"—which is how Paco got this far, James.

And all this while Chuck holds his hand over a large glass ashtray and Rita pours shot glass after shot glass of hydrogen peroxide over his raw and filthy knuckles. Chuck stares ahead and gulps his beers with extraordinary concentration. Paco watches him hold his hand stiff and steady over the ashtray, the peroxide fizzing into foam. He listens to the redneck with blank and rhetorical politeness but, intent on the blossoming pain that warms his belly and grinds into the small of his back, drinks his beer steadily down (hearing the telltale signs of the rain slacking)—not comforted at all by this respite, you understand—bleary-eyed and bus-ride tired. Suddenly he feels the firm oppression of the smell of the booze in the place; feels the rain ease and let up for good. So he gathers his gear and makes for the door, thanking the kid for the hospitality; thinking, Imagine breaking your balls for these people!

Outdoors the air is cool and humid, yet with that feeling that lets you know that the sun will soon be out. Paco walks gingerly between parked cars, intending to cross the river bridge straightaway and get into town, not three hundred paces off. He grins hard against the still-emerging, burgeoning pain rising from under the fading medication; he thinks, I have two things to do before dark, find work and get a place to stay; any damn work, hear, even chintzy damn day labor, and a place to sleep, but not a flop. I'm through with flops; through with sleeping outdoors wrapped in every shirt I own, be goddamned sure of that; through with musty, itchy barn lofts, hospitals (when they let you sleep), and shit-for-nothing, bunkhouse hostels saturated with cockroach poison.

The rich smell of rain rises all around him, well soaked into the iron-gray asphalt—the sweet overpowering aroma of dampened earth—the sparkling sheen of rain-washed foliage dazzling his eyes, the moist cool rising solidly into his shoes and sore feet. Paco walks briskly to the spindly, spidery bridge (known in the engineering trade as a Howe-type, through-truss bridge, you understand)—the asphalt roadway better than a foot thick and oozing out the runoff gutters like frozen globs of sludge. The intricate ironwork—the tension beams

and torsion beams and, overhead, trellis-looking crossbeams
—is delicate and well made. The bridge is so banged up—
pounded on and painted over, rusted up and painted again—
that the builder's plate is indecipherable and there's no telling
what year it was built. (Old man Cruikshank down at Andresen's Long Dock would tell you he was the water-bucket boy
for the crew that put it up. "The year was nineteen and aught-
four, the same year the foundry commenced to making boiler
castings, and such things, for the railroad.")

Paco would always remember this walk over the bridge,
James, with the town just beyond. Almost directly beneath, by
twenty or thirty feet, is the flood-control dam, high and thick
(built as a public-works project in the thirties). The sheet of
water, the nappe, spills over the rock-and-concrete dam from
shore to shore, rushing with an inevitable and tranquil, smooth
and unvarying silver sheen, and that constant echo-ous thrashing of thousands of gallons of water pouring furiously over
water, hypnotic and dreamlike, would always resonate in
Paco's mind. Upstream to the right as far as he can see is the
deep and broad backwater, still and shimmery as a warm
desert horizon. Maple trees and oak, sycamore and walnut and
bushy old willows droop thickly into the water. Downstream,
the river eddies over striated bedrock; splits, fanning out like a
delta among hand-sized stones and wafer-thin chips; swirls
slowly through loose gravel; joins again, straightens, deepens
to waist-high between the quarry-stone abutments of that
godawful ugly railroad bridge yonder. Then the river cascades,
sudsing, down into the woods and on through grazing pastures
sprawling with flowers, and more thickly canopied timber
woods.

That surge and swirl of water pouring over water boils

up a thick mist. Right then and there Paco feels the up-swelling chill and suddenly has an inkling—a veritable presentiment, James—of what it will feel like when he is very old.

(The boiled-up mist would produce a rainbow every once in a great long while—always on a morning when the angle of light was just right. That rainbow, as solid and superb as a Corinthian column, would sweep into the air with an easy arc and disappear into the bridge's undergirding ironwork, where flocks of bats hung and park rats nested. Sometimes a double rainbow appeared. And town boys, down at the river to hunt frogs with bow and arrow, never younger than eight or older than thirteen, would come upon the rainbows with shivering pleasure—"Hey, look at *that*," they shouted to one another, looking upward with marvel in their hearts—not always understanding the good luck of it; years later they would credit their lives of good fortune and constant windfalls to their own selfish cleverness and scrappy grit, rather than to an abundance of sheer luck, against which nothing can prevail, you understand, James.)

The low overcast overreaches the whole town and the steep wooded hills roundabout, but in another minute the sun drops below the overcast, making toward dusk and suddenly —like the crisp intake of astonished breath—a strong, clean, spring-showery light fills the street and all the air. The colors blaze—vivid bud-yellow, bright sapling-green, the deep burgundy of the bridge rust, the flat black of the fresh asphalt patches, the shimmering dazzle of the chrome trim of the cars parked up and down the street. The whole town stands before him (and us, too, James, as pleasing and dreamlike and terrifying as a discovered marvel; a haven and a conundrum)—the old row stores with large dark windows and narrow double doors, wood frame or red brick a couple of stories high, covered with dilapidated and crumbling asbestos or aluminum siding weathered through; every rusted nail, every well-worn slab of cut-stone curb, each ripple in every pane of glass, each sensuous undulation in the cloud cover, overhead; here a russet tint, there a touch of rouge or broad strokes of pink and gray, way yonder a rusty coppery color, as moist-looking as a fresh-cut fillet of Hoh River salmon.

That strong, yellowy light is squinting bright—Paco walking straight into it—and he feels its stunning warmth on his face and chest and belly, and he limps along almost imperceptibly, with his black hickory cane in one hand and that crammed-full AWOL bag (carefully folded socks, spare Levi's, extra work shirts, threadbare sweaters, shaving kit, medals, citations, and all) in his other hand, thinking to himself still, I must find work and a place to stay.

The first place he comes to is Mr. Elliot's Goods, on the left—the sign over the windows across the front dripping rust. A small placard propped up in an antique infant's high chair in the front window reads:

—Yes—
We Are
—Open—

and the screen door stands ajar, but Paco cannot see any light inside. He puts his gear aside and his face against the glass (streaked with rain) and shades his eyes with his hands. He peers in, hearing mumbling, but for the life of him can scarcely see. Through the flimsy curtains at the back of the shop he can make out a low-seated Lincoln rocker under harsh fluorescent lights, the back festooned with several spools of delicate caning; the floor is covered with newspapers and slopped with gobs of reddish paste—and behind that a jumble of woodworking tools on a tall workbench. At the front of the shop a light clicks on, so Paco takes a breath, goes in and stands by the door, and waits for his eyes to get accustomed to the dark. There is a distinct odor of turpentine and pee-soaked clothes, horn-and-hoof glue, and musty cardboard boxes filled with pulpy paperback books. The little shop is crammed to the rafters with dry-rotted steamer trunks, jumbled piles of brightly painted farmhouse furniture, slop buckets brimful of bric-a-brac, and old beer bottle boxes and bushel baskets bursting with useless, wornout kitchen gadgets. Off to the side under a glaring gooseneck lamp curled down over a high rolltop desk, Mr. Elliot sits on a high metal stool, roundly stooped over a flat pullout covered with green felt (rubbed as smooth as a chamois shirt), fiddling with the innards of a mantel clock. Many of the drawers are pulled to, revealing stacks of watch crystals, small tins of gears and springs and winding stems, trays of files and picks, tweezers and needle-nose pliers, and other well-worked jeweler's tools—the leisurely collection of a working lifetime.

And if you asked Mr. Elliot how he came to be in that little town, he'd tell you in his thick, indomitable East European accent—struggling to enunciate every vowel and consonant— "I mate boots for ze Red Ar-mee," he'd say, putting his work gently down, looking up. "Dur-rink the revolution in nine-tin hundret ant zeffen-tin ant et-tin vhen I vhas a young boy ant did not know better. I lef-fit dare plenty piss-set off vhen ze damn crooks voot not pay! I tolt zis von stink-king kommis-czar, 'You nottink but a bunch of kot-damned thee-ving Koss-

zacts. You take boots, no pay. You take food, no fuck-king pay.
Pogroms still come to my vill-letch. I piss on your revolution,
kom-rat! I spit!' So I come to zis country and open zis shop."
Mr. Elliot makes a fair living cheating the farmers at auctions
and yard sales. His real name discarded at Ellis Island, long
gone and forgotten, he answers to Mr. Henry Frazier Elliot.
"I safe all my money. Zend vor my wife—Da-rinka. She dead
now—may St. Konstance of Kiev look offer her," he'd say, and
cross himself right to left, Orthodox-fashion.

The old man bends over his desk and intently scrutinizes
his work, wearing thick glasses with a jeweler's magnifying
glass, a loupe, clipped to the gold rim and hooked down over
one eye. He tinkers with slow and elaborate patience, and
takes up the conversation with Darinka, his wife long dead—
"Zo, I says to zis city fella, Darinka, 'You just bring a big truck
ant plenty of money—all cash. I am too olt to be mess-sink
around vit checks and such non-sense. I promise you vont
be making the trip for nothing. Shus' you bring some nice
crisp cash, like a good boy!' How's dat for busy-ness, Da-
rinka?"

Then Mr. Elliot turns back to his work, waiting for Da-
rinka to answer, meanwhile rooting around in one of the shallow drawers with a long-handled tweezers for a small machine
screw. And just as Mr. Elliot takes another breath, pauses
from his work, and talks to Darinka some more, Paco raps
on the leg of the table with his cane and says, "Excuse me,
sir?" And Mr. Elliot jerks his head up and looks at Paco silhouetted like an apparition against that strong, clean, late-
afternoon light. "Eh?" the old man says, dipping his chin to
look at Paco over the rims of his glasses and the magnifying
lens.

"I'd like to talk to you about work," says Paco clearly and loudly, leaning on his cane and looking at the old man, then glancing away.

"Vork? Vork? Ah-ha, Da-rinka, zis fella's looking for vork!" the old man cries, looking up behind himself out of the corners of his eyes. "Vhat kind of vork you vant to talk about?" The old man chuckles to himself, holding up a sharply pronged timing sprocket with his tweezers, inspecting it minutely in the hard, close light of the gooseneck lamp.

Paco says, "I'm looking for anything steady," asserting his most firm and convincing voice, looking through the doorway curtains at a rocker in the middle of having its cane seat and back restored. "I can learn any sort of work you do in this shop," he assures the old man.

And Mr. Elliot—too forgetful and picky to stand anyone else's way of working—says, "Vell, let me ask you a queshun, eh? You a pretty young fella, vhy do you have that cane?" and jabs the air with his tweezers, backhanded.

Paco switches the handle of his cane back and forth a couple of times as though he's trying to screw it into the floor—half a turn at a time.

How many times is it, James, that Paco has answered that? He has dwelt on it with trivial thoroughness, condensed it, told it as an ugly fucking joke (the whole story dripping with ironic contradiction, and sarcastic and paradoxical bitterness); he's told it stone drunk to other drunks; to high-school buddies met by the merest chance (guys Paco thought he was well rid of, and never thought he'd see the rest of his natural life); to women waiting patiently for him to finish his telling so they could get him into bed, and see and touch all those scars for themselves. There's been folks to whom he's

72

unloaded the whole nine yards, the wretched soul-deadening dread, the grueling, *grinding* shitwork of being a grunt (the bloody murder aside); how he came to be wounded, the miracle of his surviving the massacre—as good as left for dead, you understand, James. "For a day and a half I thought that the very next breath I drew was going to be my last, and I was going to fucking die. And shit, what's funny is that goddamn Fire Base Harriette was supposed to be a fucking piece of cake, the same as going home and spending the night in the house where you fucking grew up—for Christ's sake," he told folks.

Paco (standing next to a table stacked with old stereoscope slides of St. Petersburg and Khartoum, Lisbon and San Francisco) immediately distills all that down to a single, simple sentence, squares himself (standing as straight as he can), looks the old man full in the face, and says bluntly, "I was wounded in the war." His body draws up, seeming to expand. (Something electric happens here, James.)

Mr. Elliot hears "wounded in the war," dips his chin again to look over his glasses—black hickory cane, workaday shoes, bleached denims, wrinkled-up shirt, and travel-tired face. There is something about the expansive timbre of Paco's voice, something about his physical presence—the old man feels Paco loom in the doorway light. And suddenly the old man is overcome by an upwelling of feeling that unleashes a deluge of memories going back fifty years and more.

The old man, then fifteen, clinging to the door handle and grab irons of a boxcar headed eastward when he deserted the Czar's army once and for all in 1917, hooking his belt around the handle for good measure, traveling for a solid week in the driving sleet and freezing rain, leaning way out

to piss and seeing the other boxcars carrying more deserters
—his shoulders swollen and sore, black and blue for weeks
afterward from the rough jostling. His seeing the troop of Red
cavalry storm into his village. Flanks of horsemeat skinned
with a pocketknife, butchered with a kindling ax, and hung
from the log rafters where he and his family ran and hid—
the bloody juice of the freshly slaughtered meat dripping into
the loose, knee-deep straw (pock-pock-pock . . .). The cavalry-
men riding bareback, with rag-wrapped feet, armed with
rifles slung across their backs like quivers; well-roughened,
bearded, and stinking-filthy from living in the woods hand-to-
mouth; knouting the bolder village men, fiercely, with short
thick whips. The soldiers spreading through the village cottage by cottage, stripping the larders bare and carrying off the
food in tow sacks. The ponies, meanwhile, shaggy as baled
cotton, stood in the creamy muck around the village well,
steaming with lathery sweat and exhaling hoarse, chugging
clouds of breath (that hung close to the ground, it was so cold).
All of those mean-spirited, angry, and sullen men looking
down, shouting and laughing as the village elders (his father
among them) counted coins—sovereigns and coppers—into
the mangy fur cap of the cavalry's commander. The cavalry-
men teased the younger children with feigned bayonet and
saber thrusts, and pawed the women—the women trembling,
with their babushkas pulled tightly around their heads and
faces, powerfully ashamed. The livestock bawled as they were
driven across the slushy snowfields to the woods. Then the
heftier troopers beheaded the village men—bound hand and
foot, kneeling and bowing, begging to be spared—murdering
them with an improvised poleax; the necks hacked at like
gnawed wood; the lopped heads rolling in the muck; the

headless corpses tipping forward and those prodigious wounds pouring blood. Winters later, the old man fled with his kit of bootmaker's tools: overland to Poland, to Germany (picking up the watchmaker's trade on the way), to England and America; on the trek out of Russia seeing many a soldier squatting cross-legged behind a machine gun or a sandbagged guardpost out in the middle of nowhere, shoulders hunched, heads down, arms and faces disappearing into a snowdrift—pockets picked clean, frozen solid like men fallen asleep in their dinner plates, the food heaped high.

Mr. Elliot—sitting on that tall metal stool behind that work desk in that little shop of his—stares off into space, remembering all that. He could easily close his eyes right here and now, and smell the hay dust sifting down through the sharp slats of sunlight coming in the chinks of the shed where his family hid on the hay mounds, terrorized for their lives. He could smell the gamy joints of meat swinging in the air, could hear the stiff rag ropes squeaking. And his confusion and heartfelt melancholy is so thorough and absolute he can only think to ask Paco one question, "What war was that, young man?"—all those memories alive in him still, twitching.

And how many times is it, James, that people have looked over at Paco, looked down, and asked, "What war was that?" as if not one word of the fucking thing had ever made the papers. And Paco answers Mr. Elliot—as simple and fretful and harmless as the old man is—the same as he nearly always answers, "Why, the Vietnam War, sir." The old man squirms around on his stool and shakes his head—he has never heard of the place—but before he can answer, Paco turns on his heel and is out the door and into the fresh air again.

"Sorry I asked," he says under his breath, meaning about the work, and pulls the screen door closed behind him.

Mr. Elliot, left staring at air, flips the loupe down over his eye again, bends the gooseneck lamp even more severely over his work, thinking in Russian, "Where was I, Da-rinka?" He looks up behind himself toward a mint-condition Singer sewing machine, the drawers stuffed with tangled attachments. But he is puzzled and troubled. "Da-rinka? Did not he look very much like Lyuba's boy, Dmitri?"

A thick steam, smelling richly of tar and scorched iron, rises from the broad, sun-warmed street in the chilly afternoon air. Paco makes his way to Hennig's Barbershop, with that warm steam rising to his knees and that gnawing, prickly itch humming like a smothered swarm around his belly and back.

Old man Elliot bobs his head, pressing a beveled timing sprocket neatly into an axle with his needle-nose pliers, and agrees with himself fully, "Yes, Da-rinka, yes," speaking loudly in Russian, "very much like Dmitri, indeed!" (Later that night at the back of the shop, where the old man lives, he will undress for bed and talk to Darinka about Paco and a dozen other things he has seen that day and imagined. He will sit on the side of his bed, sipping from a tumbler of warm whiskey. His old dog Spice—a smelly Labrador that has been asleep, virtually unnoticed, among the panels of stained glass and hand-painted china dolls—will lick the old man's purplish feet for the salt with a flat, rasping tongue. All of a sudden the old man will look up, as if someone slapped him across the top of his head—the warm fumes of the whiskey rising into his eyes and nose, smarting. And it will finally dawn on him about Paco, that kid come into the shop earlier asking about work—of all things. He will stare at a metallic lamp next to his bed in the shape of a hula dancer—her skin brown, her nipples and lips red, her eyes and hair black. The old man will blurt out, looking at the lamp, "But, Da-rinka! Dmitri, Lyuba's boy, has been dead forty-five years! That cannot be him!")

Paco walks across the way toward Hennig's Barbershop as though he were coming up to a proscenium stage—the windows are that big and the place is that well lit. Near the door a large red-and-white barber pole rotates slowly. Inside, the porcelain washbasins, the hand-crank barber chairs, and the black-and-white ceramic tile gleam and shine under bright fluorescent lights—the walls covered with cut-glass mirrors, and an old shoeshine bench at the back. Hennig—a tall, bossy-looking guy with curly, greased-back hair—likes to stand in the middle of the window as he works so he can keep track of all the comings and goings, with his feet well apart, like he's hauling water. When Paco ducked into Elliot's Goods, Hennig took one look at the severe, amateurish cut of his hair and nailed him for a GI without so much as a second glance, you understand. ("All's I got to say on that subject is this," Hennig will tell you, James, slashing the air with his scissors like a conductor's baton, "any half-bright, lard-assed nitwit who can *comb* hair can goddamn *cut* hair in the Army. All's those pissheads know is zip-zap-zip"—Hennig slashing the air with his scissors—"'*Next!*'") Hennig leisurely combs his customer's hair, dripping wet and slickered down—Hennig's hands smelling of cigars and onions and witch hazel. He circles this way and that, always working the scissors, eye-balling the guy's head like a surveyor taking the lay of the land. And the man in the chair—Mr. Holland, the haberdasher from the shopping mall west of town—sits straight-backed, earnest, and attentive, with his knees jutting up under the lap cloth draped broadly over him, mighty ill at ease, as though he's at the dentist's. Hennig works along, combing and cutting, talking to his waiting customers and snipping those scissors a couple of solid clips in the air, pointing at Paco, so that every eye in the place is on Paco by the time he is in the door (ringing a tinkling little bell hung on a bit of wire) —Holland looking at Paco severely out of the very corners of his eyes.

Hennig points to the end chair, nearest the door, directing Paco to sit there, and says, "I'll be right with you." Paco sits, sliding his AWOL bag under the chair, and loosens his jacket.

At the other end of the row sits a big, blubbery-looking guy everyone calls Russell. Everything about Russell is fat— his bushy, bristling head of hair, his flattened nose and beefy build, his short, thick marshmallow fingers, stumpy legs, and large feet. And next to him sits his equally fat and sloppy wife, Muriel ("I like 'em a little on the thick side, you know, 'cause you can get a different piece of ass every night—if you get my drift, yaw-haw-haw"). "The little woman," as he calls her, sitting there in her Hush Puppies and knee-high nylons, always comes with him to supervise his biweekly haircut, offering Hennig coaching of one kind or another, and paying him the precise amount in singles and coins— the paper always folded funny and wadded up, the coins sticky with warm, syrupy candy.

And next to Muriel is old man Cruikshank, who sells live bait down at Andresen's Long Dock. He loves to sit back of his bait shop, upriver, and admire the bridge—thinking how for

three months the whole valley could hear the iron workers
banging on the rivets with their ball peens; how goddamned
hard it was to get those last torsion beams just right; the two
men killed; and what and all. Cruikshank flips through old
copies of *Popular Mechanics* and *Field and Stream* thumbed
limp as rags.

And next to Cruikshank is Virgil Harriman, a town fire-
man, who likes to argue baseball.

After everyone has had a chance to look Paco up and
down, Hennig swings around toward Russell, pointing and
nodding slyly, priming him, you can be sure, James.

Russell scoots up in the chair and leans forward, as
though he's going to tell everyone a secret, and says (just
as though he'd been practicing all afternoon, James), "Well,
say now, you hear about that good old boy got himself killed
stone dead the other week?" Russell looks around. His wife
shoves back in her chair, crossing her legs at the ankles and
clutching her handbag, beaming. Cruikshank and Harriman
wheel around in their chairs, rolling their eyes as though they
are about to hear some outrageous lie for the umpteenth time.
Holland sits still and looks at Russell with a bright sidelong
glance, blinking hard when Hennig snips a bit of hair. And
Hennig leans way over toward Russell, coming up on his
tiptoes and shaking his head, slowly and profoundly, and
stage-whispers gladly, "Why, mercy sakes, Russell, no, I don't
recollect you ever did. What-ah-ut happened?" says he, with
profound and rhetorical astonishment.

And so Russell, keen to brag, wipes his mouth with the
back of his hand and all his fingers, spreads his hands on his
knees, and begins.

"Well," says he, "it was as true a misfortune as ever there

was." He eyes everyone up and down until he's got their attention. "One of them backcountry shines—black as the ace of spades, may I add—got himself shot stone dead in a robbery up at the Elks Club Bingo Fair. That was three weeks come Thursday. You *musta* seen it in the paper?" Hennig goes snippety-snip a couple of times, snapping at air, and shakes his head no with mild satisfaction. "Well, I am here to tell you that I have seen those guys do some plain-and-simple stupid fucking things (excuse the French, dear) in my time—and I mean some godawful dumbshit nigger stunts—but this latest episode just about takes the whole cake. This Jasper—name of Rufus or Zebedee or Snowflake, or some lame-brained affair as that—must have been a busboy or dishwasher around back in the kitchen someplace. Oh, he knew the layout of the place sure enough, but he musta been a couple bricks short of a load, because he never figured out that the Elks Club Bingo Fair is run by a couple cops' wives—yaw-haw-haw. And let me tell you, he was one surprised soul brother when he found out—yaw-haw-haw. The women, the wives—Effie Webb and Darlene Jean Miller—were sitting at a card table right around the corner from the front doors and the coatrack, counting up the evening's receipts and sorting out the door-prize stubs, sipping Wallbangers and telling dirty jokes under their breath. ('What's the difference between kinky and perverted, dearie,' says one, ducking her head behind her hand. '*Kinky* is when you use a feather, see, and *perverted* is when you use the whole chicken! Ain't that a hoot!') And right out of nowhere this jitterbug waltzed up to the card table, whipped out this pissant little .22 pistola (excuse the French, dear), and said—can you beat this—'Yo money o' yo life,' and grabbed for the cashbox, which by-the-by was just brimming with moola (they take in something like 250 smackers of a bingo night, all singles and fivers and sawbucks). Well, as I say, it sure wasn't his bingo night —yaw-haw-haw—because their husbands were standing around the corner by the coatrack, having themselves a smoke and shooting the shit (excuse the French, dear), listening to their squad-car radios over the loudspeakers with one ear and Clementine Agee calling out the bingo numbers with the other. They hear, '. . . money o' yo life,' and they jump around the hallway corner, whip out their pieces (as they call their guns) lickety-split, level them out at this dumbshit kid, say, 'Halt! Po-leese!' and before that Jasper can so much as blink and swallow his spit, they nail him with six or seven solid hits—just about tore him a new asshole, as the saying goes (excuse the French, dear)—yaw-haw-haw.

"He was as dead as a mackerel and gone to hell before he hit the wall—POW!" Russell says, and throws up his hands with a jerk, and bugs out his eyes. "And all the rest of the evening we're digging the rest of those slugs out of the wood-work. Well, sir, when the bingo players hear that commotion, they come tumbling out of the hall to gape and stare— standing there jacking their jaws—and by closing time there's blood tracked all over creation. The little woman here had to stay after, extra late, cleaning up."

Russell's wife uncrosses her ankles and leans forward in the chair, unclutching her purse. She jabs Russell in the ribs and pinches him hard on the arm, feeling snappish, and says, "*Malcolm Herbert Russell*, I *do* wish that you would learn to *modify* your language, but yes, Mr. Hennig, he is correct. There were smudges of 'dirt,' shall we say, all over the dance floor, and in the restrooms, and even at the back of the pantry, of all places, where the Elks keep the Christmas Nativity and Valentine's Day decorations."

By the time Russell finishes his story and his wife gets her two cents' worth in, Hennig is done with Holland's haircut and is stropping his straight razor as though he's swinging a scythe—you hear the sweeping tang of that honed Swedish steel with every stroke. Then Hennig helps himself to a handful of steaming lather on the back of his fingers and smears it liberally all over the back of Holland's neck and ears, slapping it on—Holland keeping track out of the corners of his eyes. Then Hennig spreads a clean towel over Holland's shoulder and commences trimming the edges of the haircut by taking a firm hold of the guy's head and leaning it this way and that. Hennig holds the razor delicately and works it around his ears and the back of his neck with short, quick strokes, wiping lather from the flat of the blade on the towel again and again, and is done in a jiffy. Everyone watches Holland's eyes dart back and forth, expressionless. They hear the razor scrape precisely across the skin, the honed steel ringing.

About halfway through the job Hennig looks at Paco and says, "And what can I do for you?"

And Paco, who right well knows loafers (and lifers) when he sees them, glances up the line at all the chairs, straightens up with his cane between his knees, watching Holland watching Hennig as he wipes the flat of the razor on the towel. Paco says, "I didn't exactly come in for a haircut."

And before Paco can say another word Russell says, "Well, what *did* you come in here for?"

Paco says, "I got put off a bus at the Texaco. I came into

town looking for work, looking for a place to stay." Do tell, thinks Russell. "Bar across the way," and Paco glances behind him in the direction of Rita's Tender Tap, "is full of traveling drunks and smart-mouth lifers. And the old guy across the street"—Paco pointing with the handle of his cane back across the street—"kept talking to someone who wasn't there—but I guess you might know a little something about that."

Everyone knows about Elliot and his dead wife, Darinka. Mr. Henry Frazier Elliot is one of those queer-looking foreigners—"Crazy as a sumbitch," as Russell would say—who talks "funny," dresses "funny," got himself into a "mighty funny business, buying up folks' stuff at farm auctions and yard sales," Russell would say. "Now what the hell sort of decent, Christian business is that?" And Mr. Elliot conducts his business "funny," as far as Russell is concerned, "selling that junk —*antiques* is what they call it, hear?—to big-city live wires. Plenty queer, that old bird, you ask me," Russell would tell you.

Harriman—a distant relation of the New York Central Harrimans—for years now one of the town's few firemen, "Best damn job *I* ever had," he'd tell you, who loafs around the stationhouse taking correspondence business courses, is teaching himself cooking and repairs kids' toys, has never troubled his head for a minute about work. Russell scrounges around, trying to make ends meet by doing passable remodeling and "home repair." Take it all around, Russell is selfish and cagey, anyway—"Nobody done me a favor" (though plenty had)—and would not tell Paco word one about work if he did hear. And Charles T. Holland, the haberdasher, has been looking Paco up one side and down the other—a veteran now, Holland thinks to himself, a veteran a body ought to help along, and he's got about the right haircut, but that cane, those roughened clothes, and that funny look in his eyes (they all got it, don't they?) wouldn't sell so much as one decent pair of shoes, ask me. Besides, a body hears too many stories as to how they got to acting so peculiar. No, Mr. Holland, he thinks to himself, best not.

Hennig pours scented witch hazel on his hands, slaps it on the back of Holland's neck, and rubs it in. Holland startles at the cold sting of it and says, "I truly wish I could help you out, young man, but I haven't heard of any work. Have you?" he turns and asks Hennig, who is finally done. Hennig unclips the lap cloth, slips it off Holland's lap, and shakes it out gently. He looks over at Russell and Muriel, old man Cruikshank and Harriman, and says, "I haven't heard of any. You?" And everyone shakes his head no. So Hennig says, "Why don't you try Boussierre's Laundry across the way. They got a message board—as a courtesy to their customers. Maybe you'll find something there. Sorry I can't help you, kid."

So before Holland hauls out his wallet to pay, before Russell gets to his feet, hitching up his trousers, and makes himself comfortable in that warm barber chair, before Muriel scooches up on the edge of her chair, Paco says his thanks and is out the door with his AWOL bag and his black hickory cane. He's out into that strong, spring-showery, yellowy light again, making his way across the street through the knee-deep steam that rises from the blacktop as thick as fur—the warmth of the blacktop seeping into his shoes, the steam cool and moist around his shins, smelling of clean rain.

Hennig stands at his cashbox fingering the money,

watching Paco closely—everyone watching Paco and having themselves a nice shit laugh, James—sure they will never see him again. "Them Vietnam boys sure do think you owe them something, don't they?"

Paco sidles between parked cars, struggling more and more with his back and legs, and smells the soap and lint, the bleach and warm moist air of Boussierre's Laundry and Dry Cleaner's. He walks through the wedged-open doors—washers along one wall, some shivering and humming, spinning dry loads of clothes. Along the other wall are twelve or fifteen dryers, rumbling—buttons and belts clacking aplenty. And in the space between are many low, wide folding tables. Four young girls with their backs to the door stand scattered among the tables, folding laundry—tending deep canvas bins of warm clothes. They don't see or hear Paco when he comes in, but stand watching a soap opera on a large television set at the back of the shop, and dip into the laundry bins every once in a while to pluck something out—socks or jock shorts, handkerchiefs, sofa-cushion covers or dress shirts. They hold each piece against their bodies, fold it deftly and quickly, and pile it accordingly on the tables in front of them. But they never take their eyes from the television, watching a distinguished-looking man in a bulky flannel shirt and heavy corduroy trousers reading a newspaper spread out on a kitchen table, spelling through the want ads with a felt-tip marker and answering the earnest questions of a mothery-looking woman busy at the sink, him giving the answers at exhaustive length, like a raconteur or a lawyer. The laundry girls watch the slowly evolving conversation with dumbfounded and steadily unblinking attention, and glance down at their work only to smooth wrinkles, check for missing buttons, and locate stray wads of lint—which they pluck up with their nails and flick into the air, like cigarette ashes.

Paco stands in the doorway, leaning on his cane more heavily than ever, James, eyeing the place for this famous bulletin board, and just that quickly those girls—the short tails of their high-school uniform blouses loose around their hips—remind him of the Viet girls at the hand-laundry whore-house at Ham Lom (Gookville, we called it), across the road from Fire Base Harriette. Every day in the late afternoon the laundry was hauled by the basketful from our base camp at Phuc Luc to the village—and many another village in that neck of the woods—in those three-wheeled Lambrettas and Hondas. Paco, and the rest of us, too, James, would sprawl on the warm, rugged roof of a perimeter bunker of a morning (that roof as thick as you are tall) and watch the laundry girls across 135–150 meters of flat and open ground with Lester's (the company sniper's) field glasses. The whores (all fifteen and sixteen and seventeen, you understand) worked with their loose-fitting pants rolled to their crotches, their tight-fitting blouses unbuttoned and loose, and their long black hair pulled back and done up in tight buns under their broad cone hats—their bodies gleaming with sweat and their small breasts jiggling and swaying petitely. They would wash the loads of clothes—GI fatigue uniforms and civilian R&R duds —in huge tubs, sloshing the sudsy water around the hooch yard, then drop the steaming, dripping-wet clothes on a sprawling bamboo rack in the burning-hot sun to dry. And watching the whores work, James, never failed to provoke our hard-ons.

Paco soon discovers the bulletin board in the corner almost hidden behind the Coke machine. The notes are scrib-

bled and handprinted and typed on 3 x 5 cards, scraps of
envelope, and soapbox cardboard, then tacked to the dark
cork with pushpins and thumbtacks, straight pins and small
finishing nails.

And the thing reads something like this:

A N N O U N C E M E N T S :

Jaycees Fishfry every Friday evening.
Come one. Come all. All you can eat.

Need a ride to Detroit, bad.
Will share driving, buy gas.

Sanctified Freedom Hall Fellowship.
Meet Jesus. Get saved! Free will
offering. Praise the Lord!

F O R   S A L E :

'56 Chevy. A clean machine. Mint
condition. Partly customized. See
it and believe it.

Baled hay by the truckload or the bale.
Fodder, mulch, mobile home insulation.

Three bedroom house with well-tended
organic garden. Lots of rhubarb and asparagus.
Retiring to Florida, finally.
Right family gets right price. (SOLD)

Industrial engineered washers and dryers.
Well used but cheap. See proprietor.

Have full line of Amway, including
vitamins and other health and beauty
aids. Buy now and save. Call Russell.

FOR HIRE:

Will babysit in your home. Day or night.
When you're out you want the best in.
Call Thelma or Beulah.

Expert hair care. Will call at your
home.

Truck for hire—Cash Only—Also well-
seasoned firewood by the cord.
Will deliver.

Roto-till any size lot. By the hour.
$20 minimum. Call for details.

Odd jobs. Capable of anything. Hefting
and toting my specialty. Call Russell now.

Will dowse and drill your well. Dowsing
guaranteed. References ready. We'll hit
good water or you don't pay.

Vehicle repair. All kinds. Body work
too. I can fix anything. All work
guaranteed.

Spring cleaning, quick and easy. Floors,
windows, basements, garages, attics,
expert landscaping. I haul the trash.
Tell me what you need. Say, don't delay,
call Russell today!

HELP WANTED:

Man or boy who knows dairy business.
Pay on shares, room and board.

Companion to come into my home and
attend my invalid aunt. Clean, well-
spoken, pleasant reading voice. A
churchgoing high-school girl will
do nicely. Call in person and have
Christian references in hand.

Give away free promotional samples and
nationally advertised personal
hygiene products over the phone
in your spare time at home. This is
no gimmick. Only serious and eager,
success-oriented men and women need
apply.

Daily work. Daily pay. Work when
you want. Flexible skills good,
but many non-skill jobs too. Queue
forms in Rita's lot at 5 a.m. sharp,
except Sundays.

And that was about it.

Paco rubs his eyes and face, thinking to himself, My man, you'd think there'd be more than this. Fuckin' dipstick little towns. Why didn't I have another couple bucks to make it to the next town? (Paco had given the driver all the money in his pocket and said, "Let me off when the money runs out," and the carfare had lasted all the way to the Texaco station.) Worse come to fuckin' worst, I'll queue up at Rita's for day labor—I've sure as shit done more fucked-up work than that. He turns and walks back into the street, the sun as warm as ever and the steam rising thickly to his knees.

He crosses to the drugstore and goes into the back under the hard, bright fluorescent lights, where the pharmacist stands behind a shoulder-high counter. Paco asks the man for a job, telling himself, I can handle a cash register; I know how to handle money; anybody can peddle papers and magazines, cigarettes and notions and such. But the pharmacist leans over the high counter, looking down at Paco between placards of Alka-Seltzer and stacks of packets of condoms, and can tell right away that Paco is on downers, James, and calculates that, if he puts that kid behind the counter up front, his trade would drop off 35 percent in ninety days.

"I am sorry," he says, and turns away, rifling through the drawers looking for something to do. "I have nothing. No."

So Paco turns stiffly on his heel—the warm grinding pain coming into his belly with steady beats, like the furling of a pennant in a good hard breeze. He is outside into the cool moist air and warm sun, and across the street in no time and in the door of an auto-parts place. Fan belts and radiator hoses hang down from everywhere—the place smelling of new rubber and clean oil. "I'm looking for work," he tells the clerk—the guy with a clipboard of invoices under one arm and parts boxes in the other. "You try up at the foundry?" the guy says, ducking down an aisle, muttering, "Tappet springs, tappet springs. Where are those E–44 tappet springs. Ah-ha!" And he grabs a box, coming back toward the counter. "You try up at Rita's?"

"Yeah," says Paco, "but I worked all the day-labor jobs I'm going to in this life." And the clerk slows down, coming up the aisle and thinking to himself, I don't know why these goddamn drifters get so fucking picky—job's a job, man. You do it and punch out and go home and don't think another thing about it; it's *all* shit as far as I'm concerned.

Then the guy disappears down another aisle, looking for valve cover gaskets, tailpipe clamps, and plastic license-plate screws.

Instantly, Paco is across the street and in the door of an insurance agent—the only office on the street with the heat on. The knee-high radiators gurgle and clank. Jaycee softball league trophies and glittering sales award plaques cover the walls. The place is as close and quiet as a library, and the woman behind the desk nearest the door sips hot lemony tea, ticking the names off a phone list with a very sharp pencil. She has her feet curled this way and that behind the modesty panel, exercising her toes.

"Yes, young man?" she says when Paco comes in, setting off a pleasant little buzzer. "Can I help you?"

Paco stands as straight as he can and asks for work.

"Well, young man," she says, sitting back in her chair, giving Paco a leisurely once-over the same as everyone else in town. "I really don't know of any. Did you ask Mr. Hennig at the barbershop? There's usually something listed at Boussierre's on the bulletin board, contract labor and so forth." She considers Paco's voice—she solicits over the phone, selling kitchen hardware, magazine subscriptions, and insurance deals. As she listens to Paco talk she decides that he would not do very well—there's a six-phone boiler room at the back, James. "Did you ask at the McDonald's out at the shopping center? *We* are not presently looking for associates, and we don't usually hire unless the applicant has references from another agency and a good deal of experience in the insurance and real-estate field. I'm sure you understand. I am sorry we can't help you," says she, and with that takes up her tea and pulls the pencil out of her hair.

Not a breath later Paco is out on the sidewalk again with the last of the runoff rattling the downspouts—spring-showery, yellowy light full in his face, squinting-bright. He stands at the corner of the curb and looks over the rest of the town. Kitty-corner across the street is a greasy-spoon restaurant called the Texas Lunch, with a wedge-shaped, copper-covered marquee over the doorway and tall storefront windows, heavily steamed over, dripping with condensation. Across from the Texas Lunch—across the broad, bricked railroad alley from Paco—is the Geronimo Hotel, with its broad and generous porch, and folding chairs and wicker chairs, where the old-timers and loafers (like old man Cruikshank) sit with wrists draped over their knees and heads bowed, sunning their arthritis, gossiping and bitching and spitting worked-up chew into the street. In one window is a plain sign that reads:

> ROOMS
> DAY, WEEK
> OR MONTH
> (*See Earl*)

and in another window a neon sign reads:

> *Earl & Myrna's*
> HUSTLE ON INN
> *Beer & Good Snacks*

Back across the street is Savic and Sons, a Ma and Pa hardware store if there ever was one, James, with coin purses and mittens and whatnot clipped to a long string, hanging in the front window—lost and found. Then back on Paco's side of the street behind the Geronimo Hotel is the all but abandoned train station. Straight up the street are plain brick bungalows set back from the road, an old A&P supermarket now called Clarence's Clothing Clearance Closet, a dime store, and more bungalows hidden by thick lilac and hydrangea hedges. To the right of the Texas Lunch the town's one good hill rises with ready steepness, ringed with contoured side streets and more houses. Paco luxuriates in the warm and rich, pungent smell of the tarry asphalt that rises from the street—that and the sweet aroma of grease and salt. He stares hard at the Texas Lunch (someone rubbing a spot of glass clear with a handful of napkins), calculating how much money he has (and he knows to the penny, James)—one dollar and forty-six cents: four quarters is a dollar; three dimes is a dollar-thirty; and three nickels is a dollar-forty-five; and that one penny makes it forty-six.

He crosses the intersection obliquely, moving from that strong, clean light—glaring bright—into the chill shade, which tingles his face but is easy on the eyes. And he keeps his eyes on the tall double doors. In the watered-over window on one side is the name of the place, TEXAS LUNCH, and in the other window, EAT LUNCH, with a small cardboard sign that says, TEX-MEX CHILI. Paco quickly figures that he has about enough money for a bowl of chili and some oyster crackers (these places always give you a side bowl of crackers) and a couple cups of coffee—something to get him warm and keep him going. A bright maroon Jaguar XKE convertible, fire-engine-maroon, is parked right at the curb in front, up to its doorhandles in steam. Paco glances inside as he passes— water puddled in the ashtray, a dripping-wet sweater balled up on the passenger's side, along with a pair of thong sandals. Rain-soaked cigarettes and sunglasses, scratch pad and blue Bic pen, dashboard compass and tortoise-shell combs, and a lady's alligator wallet. The crankcase clicks, cooling down. He makes the curb and walks in underneath the copper-covered marquee—discolored to that distinctive, powdery lime tint. And all this happens in an instant, as Paco walks those twenty-five paces—the fierce, flat-slanted sun, the pungent steam so thick you would think his legs were cut off at the knees, the smell of food that starts his belly churning. Just as he gets to the iron-edged stoop, the warm blast of air coming through the tall double doors lifts the hair of his head and fills his wind-breaker, and when Paco steps through the doorway into the Texas Lunch, it is as though he's walked into someone's kitchen. Paco looks wan and drawn, his face colorless and his whole body tingling. He chooses one of the middle stools along the linoleum counter, hooks his cane on the edge, and slides his AWOL bag under him. A young woman sits at the counter near the door with a cup of coffee in front of her, her rain-soaked shorts and hockey jersey clinging tightly—killing time; hers is the XKE parked at the curb and the varicolored sweater. Behind the counter is an old crank cash register and an iron-gray griddle, a four-burner gas stove and an Anets steam table, a four-slice toaster and a deep fryer (the grease crackling hot), and a closet-sized walk-in freezer. Way at the back and in plain sight of everyone is the dishwasher's station— the Texas Lunch is too small for a machine, you understand, so all the dishes are done by hand. A hatchet-faced guy bends over the large, stainless-steel, double-tub sink (identical to any U.S. Army mess hall back sink in the continental United States, James), muttering and singing, and chucking stacks of dishes and special platters into the tub brimming with hot water and frothy suds.

Ernest Monroe, the owner of the place, stands behind the counter, sneaking a smoke near the door to the walk-in ("Bought this here place from a couple of Greeks; beats the shit out of me how two guys like that come to own a place with a name like Texas Lunch, but there they were and here I am," he'll tell you, James). He watches Paco virtually burst in the place and make a straight wake for the middle of the counter. He fully recognizes Paco's 1,000-meter stare, that pale and exhausted, graven look from head to toe. Ernest drops his smoke into a wet can of garbage, picks up a menu from the rack behind one of the napkin dispensers dotted up and down the counter, gives it to Paco, and pours him a glass of water, which Paco drinks right down (thirsty and dehydrated). Ernest pours him another glass, which he also drinks, so Ernest pours him another, which Paco sips.

"Coffee?" Ernest asks, knowing well enough that whatever else these guys can afford—sometimes only a muffin, sometimes a slice of pie, sometimes a big steak-and-eggs breakfast no matter the time of day—whatever else they ask for, they always want coffee. Paco nods, staring at the kettle of chili on the stove, its sides slopped with streaks of deviled beef. Ernest wipes his hands on his apron, worn doubled and redoubled as thick as padding around his middle, and serves Paco his coffee—the mug one of those comfortably rounded, thick-handled numbers you used to see in roadhouse cafeterias. Paco scans the single sheet of menu up and down, intent on finding the price of the chili before he asks about the oyster crackers (sometimes they're extra). He pours half an inch and more of milk into the mug (called Boston coffee, James) and a steady stream of sugar, teaspoon after heaping teaspoon.

"How much is the chili?" Paco asks, not finding it on the menu after all, but eyeing the kettle—ready now to promise anything to get rid of the gnawing, grinding ache in his gut.

Ernest turns aside and takes hold of the long-handled ladle, stirring it deeply into the kettle. The chili steams and gurgles. "A bowl of my homemade Tex-Mex chili—which will stick to your ribs without a doubt—*and* coffee, goes for the princely sum of a dollar-seventeen, if you skip the tip. Comes with oyster crackers and a big spoon. Warm you up plenty. Want some?"—Paco nods, grateful—"More water!" which Paco does not gulp but nevertheless drinks straight down. Ernest serves the chili (spiced beef with chilis, cumin, garlic, paprika, oregano, and only cornflour for thickener—no beans, no pasta, no nothing else, mind you), setting the bowl under Paco's nose. The stunning aroma of those sweet, hot spices rises into his face—his eyes tingle; his mouth waters. He crushes a fistful of oyster crackers and sprinkles the crumbs over the chili, which is so simmering hot that a skin forms over the top, like the skin on warm milk in a cool glass. Ernest stands near him, wearing heavy oxfords spotted with white, starchy potato juice. Monroe is a big man, his own best customer, with knife cuts and grease burns across the back of his hands; drives a mint-condition, cream-puff 1948 Mercury, and is a WWII Marine. ("Tell you one thing, young man, once a goddamned United States Marine, always a fucking Marine").

Paco bends over his bowl of chili, eating slowly, savoring it, the food *hot* in his mouth: adding more and more crackers, drinking down glass after glass of cold water, working on his dehydration, sipping mugfuls of Boston coffee laced with many teaspoons of sugar. And just now that strong, clean, spring-showery. yellowy light streaks straight in the back door (a sudden sharp presence that makes everyone blink, startled) lighting up everything—industrial cookware, black iron burners, spatula and spoons rubbed clean from use—the wooden handles gleaming with the sheen of patina. The strong, clean light is also reflected from the buildings across the street, the shimmering glare streaming in the watered-up windows the same as bright sunlight through a muddy windshield, and it seems to intensify the smell of the street—the XKE's crankcase; the sun-scorched asphalt, steaming up and rain-freshened.

Paco eats, finally clearheaded, remembering the rain (feeling the dampness in his shoes); Ernest Monroe, pulling out another smoke and commencing his argument with Peterson, the dishwasher, remembers how the rain blew in the doors. And that young woman—her name Betsy Sherburne, James—sits on the stool nearest the door, with one foot hooked under her, chewing the ends of her ponytail and playing with her coffee mug and ring of keys—eyeing Paco, you can bet, James, intrigued; attracted, no doubt—remembering right well what it was like racing through the cold downpour coming in from Griffin.

Now, at the same time the mechanic and Paco walked into Rita's Tender Tap, Betsy, coming from the other direction in her fire-engine-maroon Jaguar XKE convertible coupe, overtook the downpour that overtook the whole town. The front came through, the temperature dropped fifteen degrees, and there she was—it was like driving *into* night (that's how dark it got, James). She had the top down—"Too late now, son-of-a-bitch!"—the radio going full blast and the heater on high to keep her legs warm. She cruised into town, pulled to the curb at the bottom of the hill in front of the Texas Lunch, leaped out—it was still raining cats and dogs, mind you—and ran inside on her tiptoes, with her clothes absolutely plastered to her body. And even Ernest, who's known Betsy nearly all her life—old enough to be her father—had to admit that seeing her come dashing in his place with her soaked-through clothes clinging to her body like that made his groin stir.

Right this moment, James, we could stand in the middle of the street at the edge of the shadow of that bright, late-afternoon light, with the last of the runoff dripping quickly on lean-to side roofs as fast as a drumroll; dripping on slick, mildewed wood as loud as hand slaps. We could stand in that warm steam—our legs moist to the knees—and look over the burled rosewood dashboard and the swept-down hood of

Betsy's XKE and watch her leaning over her coffee and her keys, feeling angry and happy at the same time; killing time, with her eyes dazzled by that clean light and her body distinctly silhouetted. Her luxurious head of hair is soaking wet, done in a thick and furry ponytail—looking tinted or frosted from this distance; a loose wreath of hair matted to her forehead and neck; her high-school hockey jersey and well-washed denim cutoffs uncomfortably clinging. We can stand in the cool shadow of that strong, clean, spring-showery, yellowy light, James, and snap!—just that quickly Betsy has never been more beautiful than she is right now, and will never be so again.

If we could somehow take this whole image—the moist, aromatic steam rising to our knees, the water-beaded XKE, the neat and gracious curve of the windshield opposing the elegant curve of the sloping-down hood, the smell of well-worked, hot machinery, and the wet, expensive upholstery leather; the ramshackle porch and felt-green copper marquee overhead; the blunt glare of hard light coming in the back door—Paco silhouetted harshly, too—crisscrossing with the clear and peculiarly ambient light reflected from the buildings across the street through the farmhouse screen door and the water-streaked windows and bright-blue checkered café curtains; Betsy's face and body moist and cool, like well-thumbed polished bronze (with a distinct wet-weather, wet-leather smell about her); the hard sparkle of the kitchen cookware; the rich smells of spiced chili, salty pickles, the dishware tainted with bleach from the rinse water; the mottled spirals of gummy flystrips hanging from the high ceiling like stalactites; and the crisp odor of thick frost on the windows of the walk-in cooler; all this together with Betsy's voluptuous sensuality—if this whole, full image could be seized and frozen —not just photographed, mind you, not simply filmed—we could hold this image up, years hence, James, and look around among ourselves and say, "How beautiful she was!"

And this moment is not lost on Paco, mind you. Betsy is nobody's angel, you understand—"Hussy," her mother has called her to her face. Most of the young-blood pilgrims down at Rita's have enjoyed her plenty, calling her the "town punch-board," and bragged about how mighty fine is her pussy—"Eatin' pussy, sure," the guy with the Adam's apple has said.

It was Betsy who took a handful of cheap paper napkins and cleared a spot on the windows—wiping at the condensation until the napkins were a gob of pulp—watching Paco zigzag up the steamy street toward the Texas Lunch, watching Paco lean more and more heavily on that black hickory cane of his.

She sits clammy and chilly on that first stool, thinking how nice it would be to sleep with Paco, getting him drunk and taking him home, where they would fuck on that sofa bed in the side den (her folks on one of their annual world cruises); her thinking that the next morning he would wake first, shower in the maid's bedroom, and stand on the threshold of the screened-in porch, looking out over the huge, silver clusters of flowers on the hydrangea hedge down toward the river. And the early-morning light is reflected up the slope, under the trees (Paco's line of sight identical with the angle of light). And those squiggly, wiggly, rippled reflections of water spread across the ceiling of the sun porch—the sparkle keen in Paco's face.

Betsy imagines all this in the harsh, after-storm light of the Texas Lunch. And, too, she imagines the swirled-around scars up and down his back, and how they disappear over his shoulder and up into his hairline; how she would lay her head on his shoulder and stroke the scars of his belly (watching his cock rise, pulling at it with her fingertips as if she were smoothing a feather), the pink and purple scars going every which way—Paco's belly strong and hard, the scars not smooth (she *feeling* his heart's beat). She sees herself drawing on his scars as if they were Braille, as if each scar had its own story. Betsy sits there with one leg drawn up under her, chewing the tip of her ponytail, and imagines she and Paco becoming lovers, but it is an impulse that neither of them acts upon, James, as many times that summer as they casually encounter each other.

The color has come back into Paco's face; his cheeks flush, his belly feels, finally, whiskey-warm—what with all that spicy chili and hot coffee. He finally looks up, puts the spoon down, and asks for more coffee yet. Ernest fills his coffee again, and looks at the two of them—Paco sitting at one end of the counter and Betsy at the other—and he wants to laugh. But in that instant he realizes food and Betsy are not all that's on Paco's mind, and before Paco can say a thing, Ernest turns to the dishwasher at the back, "Hey, you, Peterson! Drop that work and hustle down to Elliot's place and see if he's got my rocker ready yet." The guy drops another armload of dishes into the sudsy, hot wash water, whips off his apron (smeared with garbage) with the next motion, turns, and is out the wide back doorway in a huff.

Paco stretches his back, wanting something to sit against, but feeling warm and revived. He pulls a wrinkled pack of smokes from his flannel shirt and lights one.

Ernest comes forward with the coffeepot again, warming

his cup. "You know how to work a back sink?" he asks, swinging the Pyrex back in that direction. Betsy turns and watches
the two of them.

"How much does it pay?" Paco asks, feeling he has to be
cagey.

"I'm paying that guy two dollars an hour, but he's piss
poor. I'll pay you two and a quarter. If you work out, we'll up
it to three. We open at 6 a.m. and close at 11 p.m., six days a
week. You come in around ten-thirty, eleven in the morning,
bus dishes, wash anything that moves, maybe wait tables if
we get busy. Nothing complicated, just ask them what they
want and tell me. If they don't want nothing that's on the
menu, tell them to take a hike out to the Hogadorn place and
talk to 'Razzberry' at the Apocalypse. After closing, you clean
everything up, scrub it, and stow it away. Lock up usually
around midnight. Got a place to stay?" Paco is going to say
no, but before he moves a muscle Ernest says, "You go across
the street to Earl and Myrna's, and tell them you're working
for me. It's decent and clean, and close enough you can sleep
plenty late." He sidesteps down to the cash register near where
Betsy sits, cranks it open, and takes out a twenty. "Here's a
couple bucks in advance. Give it to Earl on account. Right?"

"Yeah, thanks," Paco says, his back crackling with ache.

"Good," says Ernest. "Two and a quarter it is. The eats are
on me, so long as you don't eat me out of house and home.
One question, though," he finally asks—Betsy listening, too
—"what's the cane for?"

Paco sniffs, looking at the kitchen-knife scars on the back
of Ernest's hands, takes up the mug of coffee, and luxuriates
in the radiating, almost painful warmth of it, looks down at
the pleasing curve of the handle, the crackled texture of the

hickory grain, and says, "I was wounded in the war." The pain of his body sharp and clean, bristling, from the tip of his head to the bottoms of his feet.

Betsy jerks her head around as if pinched—looks away and down, knocks her keys against her coffee. All she can think about are those scars on the back of his neck, like a piece of ordinary kitchen wax paper balled up, then spread out and smoothed flat, the paper crackling.

"Me too," says Ernest, and points to the dark, crescent-shaped scar on his right chest under his T-shirt.

"Well. See you in the morning. About ten-thirty, you say," Paco says, and Ernest nods. Paco takes the money and puts it in his jacket pocket, flips up his cane, and picks up his AWOL bag—Ernest saying, "See you in the morning, hey!"; Paco saying, "Thanks for the job!"—and leaves. He crosses the street to the Geronimo Hotel, quickly arranges with Earl, a red-faced Irishman, for a room upstairs, takes a long warm shower in the bathroom at the end of the hall, gobbles down his bedtime dose of anti-depressants and muscle relaxers, and goes to bed without so much as unpacking his gear.

5. The Texas Lunch.

Now, this may not have anything to do with our story, James, but you can always tell the class of a place by the look of the menu they give you.

First there's the open-air hot-dog stand, where the menu is displayed on huge opaque plastic panels above an elbow-high plywood counter; the whole place is besmirched with years of cooking grease, smelling of spilled lemonade, and dusted with sand blown across the boardwalk from some crummy resort beach. A chuckleheaded, no-talent cook shovels food around a burned-out griddle with a warped spatula in one hand and a beat-up barbecue fork in the other, pouring sweat into the food for all to see. The condiments—bright-red ketchup and iridescent yellow mustard—come in those gallon jugs with the squeeze-down squirt tops, and the runny pickle relish is served out by the great dripping dollop with an Ekco-brand gravy ladle, hammered flat.

Then there is the menu from the restaurant with decent fountain service and a neighborhood walk-in clientele that positively thrives on its brisk phone-order pizza business; it has a softball team, and is run like a top by three immigrant brothers, with considerable help from their doughy little mother and a couple of non-English-speaking great-uncles. The uncles toil good-naturedly in the kitchen ("It beats the shit out of the old country," they'd tell you if they could), singing Caruso arias and spitting chew on the floor. They grunt and sweat and fart, and swear lustily in Neapolitan Italian, especially when the county health inspectors come snooping around, calling the inspectors goddamned ignorant, ugly bastard sons of sheep-stealing bitch mongrel dogs—grinning and winking at each other as they hop and whoop around the kitchen making pizzas by hand. The waitresses, all older women, come to work tricked out head to toe in childishly preposterous uniforms, a cross between meter maids and registered nurses; and raggedy old black guys wash the dishes and superintend the more dip-stick relatives, who bus dishes, haul the garbage, and work the fountain. The food is the same straight vanilla, greasy-spoon bill of fare as the Texas Lunch—the same exact food, mind you, James—but here the menu is as big as a tabloid newspaper, as stiff as a shirt cardboard, and reads like a train schedule. A short snappy narrative describes every little thing as succulent, piping hot, tangy, or chewy; the coffee is famous, the refills endless; and everything else has a *satisfying* aroma, is *zestful, healthful, robust!*

There are thousands of these restaurants, James, each with its own schmaltzy gimmick. One has a gleaming, well-lit, 300-gallon aquarium with a coral reef and a shipwreck, teeming with pricelessly ugly tropical fish. Another has really hand-some singing waiters dressed fit to kill in Lederhosen, bright shirts, and light-up bow ties, better known for their Tyrolean *a cappella* than their service. Still another has walls plastered with dime-a-dozen fake Currier and Ives prints and antique ship models (evoking a clubby, Ivy League air), and a sentimental weakness for something called "sticky buns" (pecan rolls to the rest of us, James) and metallic-tasting, flaming desserts they serve with the deliberate, bumptious pomp of Hugh Griffith, say, broadly clowning his way through *Tom Jones*—"Good God! Stand thee back! [Whoosh!] Look at that, bucko!" Then there is the place with the show-off amateur actor for a cook, who wears a starched white tunic with a bright-blue kerchief and stands on a raised platform behind the broiler in plain sight of everyone. He skids back and forth behind an enormous grill—the sparkling grease smoke sucked straight up into a roaring exhaust blower—flipping marinated parts ("Chicken!"), grossly overcooked cuts of steak ("Meat!"), and slabs of ribs as long as your arm ("Ribs, *baby!*").

Then there's the sort of place where the menu comes with its own waiter, the pages loosely bound with a gold cord tied in a tassel that dangles in your lap—the wine list bound separately, like an album of wedding pictures. The waiters here used to be Parisian, then they were Prussian, now they are just as likely to be Persian or Basque or Vietnamese. The pianist (by the name of Horst, or some such) sits behind an ebony baby grand in a black suit and frayed clip-on bow tie, like a chauffeur, "tickling the ivories" and happily taking requests from the diners. And for that purpose there is a brandy snifter as big as a samovar with a couple of tens and fivers stuffed in significantly to give the patrons the broadest possible hint. And the food—Half a Chicken at Room Temperature in Tarragon Sauce *or* A Paillard of Veal *or* Every Day a Stew or Ample Pot Full of Soup—the food, James, is prepared in a steaming-hot basement kitchen both spotless and well rigged, as noisy and busy as a three-alarm fire. The chef—a foul, beefy Spaniard—wears his chef's hat squashed flat, like a mushroom, and his tunic with most of the buttons undone, so the kitchen women can see his hair. He straddles a big stool, sipping glasses of bitter black tea or cheap red wine, and supervises the second-rank cooks with a loud and rasping voice and a big pair of tongs, snapping and pinching the ones he can reach— "Scald, you dolt, *then* simmer . . . Slice, slice, slice, chop, chop, chop . . . More garlic, Renni, you simpleton, then wash your hands . . . Stir deep this broccoli, you drunkard . . . *Sprinkle*, sprinkle that cheese like you were counting dimes out of your hand with your thumb and first finger, so . . . Throw this sauce out! You trying to poison me, you worm? And zip your zipper and straighten your trousers, this is *not* the Holiday Inn!"

Then there is the small-town, lunch-counter greasy spoon —like the Texas Lunch—where the menu is a single, well-thumbed sheet of erasable bond typing paper slipped into an acetate and black plastic cover, with a little metal clip sewn into the stitching for the Special-of-the-Day cards. The menus are kept in those rack-looking contraptions along the back edge of the linoleum counter behind the napkin dispensers and salt and pepper shakers. Across the top of a greasy-spoon menu is a simple list that goes something like this:

Soup of the Day   Juice   Salad

and at the bottom of the page under the all-inclusive category of Dessert is:

Ice Cream
Sherbet
Pie
Cake
Fruit Cup

And spread out in the middle of the page you'll find everything else:

Hamburger
Hamburger, with Everything
Hamburger, with Everything, Including
    French Fries or Home Fries

and such as that. (And don't you know, James, that everything *means* everything—store-bought ketchup, stone-ground Brazilian mustard, slices of Early Girl tomatoes instead of those cumbersome wedges, sweet pickles, and iceberg or Blackseed Simpson lettuce.) And when you walk into the place, you know right away what the soup of the day will be, because the brimful pot is there on the side grill next to the toaster and the deep fryer, with that long-handled ladle encrusted with split pea or cream of mushroom, or what have you.

Now, in the town of Boone there are two restaurants: the Apocalypse, a vegetarian commune west of town on the old Hogadorn place, and the Texas Lunch, at the bottom of the town's hill, across the way from the Geronimo Hotel.

At the Apocalypse the most popular item on the menu is something called Soybean Surprise, a thick, lumpy, grayish gruel made with Yucatán soy, homemade tofu, a big handful of garden herbs, and some sort of viscous vinegary curd, all of which is heated together nearly to a boil and left to simmer for many hours, smelling up the place like a 20-gallon bucket of Korean kimchee. The cook—the owner and operator—a fat, jolly old hippie everyone calls "Razzberry," with a beard as big as an inner tube and a head of hair that hangs down in squiggly dreadlocks, loves to parade and prance around the dining room in his Lee overalls, James, exhorting the customers and free-loaders, "Eat! *Eat!* Tomorrow we die!" while taking hits of whipping cream from an aerosol can of Reddi Wip, instantly filling his squirrel cheeks and bugging his eyes. (Reddi Wip sounds like sudsy water being sucked down a drain, like the honk of many geese.)

The other place is the Texas Lunch, owned and operated by Ernest Monroe, a World War II Guadalcanal Marine who also fought on Iwo Jima. ("Guadalcanal about broke my fuck-ing balls," he'll tell you, James, especially after he's had a couple tumblers of the sweet, homemade rosé wine he makes in the basement, "but Iwo Jima was my goddamned declaration of independence.") The Texas Lunch has high and wide store-front windows, blue-and-white-gingham café curtains, a high ceiling covered with those old-fashioned panels of pressed tin, a dozen stools along the counter, and half a dozen four-chair tables covered with yellow oilcloth. And the Specials of the Day are as plain as plain can be, James—beans and franks one day, liver and onions the next; baby back ribs, lasagna, Tex-Mex chili, corned-beef hash, in-season smelt, sweet pep-pers stuffed with lamb and rice, Thuringer and German potato salad—but you get a workingman's portion in a workingman's town, and no one much complains.

· · ·

That first night in town Paco sleeps for twelve hours straight through, and wakes in the full light of day feeling fine, considering; ready for work. He washes up, dresses in clean clothes, and just after ten crosses the street. Ernest quickly shows him the bus-pan stations, the back of the kitchen, the rinky-dink back sink (as he calls it, James), and vaguely explains the scheme of the place, then leaves Paco to figure it out and fend for himself. Besides, there is cooking to do.

Now, James, in reference to some scenes shortly to be described, and for the best understanding of all similar scenes that take place in the Texas Lunch, let's settle this matter of how Paco washes dishes by hand.

He arrives through the back door, hangs his cane on a nail at the side of the shelf near the radio, and dons his apron—a broad linen thing with a neck loop and long tie strings that he doubles up and redoubles around his waist. The place is still only half busy. He fills the washtub sinks, pouring two heaping cups of industrial lye soap into the deep right-hand tub, and two or three cups of commercial laundry bleach into the left-hand tub, filling them about two-thirds full with piping-hot water—as hot as he can stand. (County health regulations specify that a rinsing bath with a weak solution of "very hot potable water and bleach will be used, followed by ample air drying to preclude handling.") Then he pours himself a cup of Boston coffee with plenty of sugar, and collects the brimming-full bus pans, now and again bumping into his cane, setting it a-swinging.

The Texas Lunch customers eat in three distinct waves, and there are *always* dishes to wash. Ernest opens at six and cooks breakfast for the day shift on its way to work, then for the swing shift and night crews coming off. The middle of the afternoon, he serves the p.m. shift going on and the a.m. shift coming off, and lastly, late in the evening, he serves dinner to the graveyard shift—the swing shift, some call it—coming back on. This in addition to the regular hours for ordinary breakfast, lunch, and dinner.

Paco would gather the bus pans on the right-hand drain-board, then stack the glassware, the coffee mugs, and the dishes (scooping the garbage into the old banged-around galvanized-iron garbage can next to him—using his hand as a cupped claw), while dumping the flatware into the washtub of lye soap to soak on the floor underfoot next to the grease trap.

First and foremost to wash are the glassware and the dozen and more coffee mugs. He takes down the bottle washer —a heavily weighted gadget with two long, thick-bristled brushes—and drops it into the washtub. Then, taking a breath—the water is *piping* hot, remember—he takes two glasses at a time, shoves them down on the brushes, gives them a couple of quick twists, douses them a time or two in the rinse (where the sweet, slimy odor of bleach rises into the air and fills his head), and sets them down in orderly rows on the left-hand drainboard (lined with a gummy, flexible rubber mesh). The whole washtub contraption is hot to the touch, mind you, James—Paco, leaning over the washtub and rinse, gets the heat right in his crotch and belly; he has a habit of standing on a Pepsi-Cola carton to keep out of the sloppy wet and hooking his belt buckle over the curved lip of the tubs to help with the balance. But this first hot wash is always the worst—a son-of-a-bitch, "Just a motherfucker," Paco would tell you, James, ready to show you the raw skin of his arms, "but I've been worse off, so it ain't no sweat." And by the time he's half done with the glasses and mugs, there's another round of bus pans to fetch—this without having touched a dish yet—the morning crowd beginning to thin down. So Paco circumnavigates the room again, picking these up one by one, pausing to refill coffee mugs and clear away dishes from the counter. The work is sloppy but methodical—everything has a place, James, and everything *in* its place—the glasses and mugs washed right away, rinsed and set out to drain-dry two by two, the dishes stacked, the flatware dropped into the washtub underfoot to soak, and the first of the cook pots and pans doused with water and sprinkled with kitchen cleanser.

When he's done with the glasses, out comes that long-bristled gadget, and in go the stacks of special platters, the ordinary dinner plates, the side-order saucers, the cereal bowls, more coffee mugs, the tin creamers, the butter dishes and dessert plates—as many as will fit. A minute's soaking in that washtub is usually enough for any dish, James—Paco fetching another bursting-full bus pan of dishes in the meantime, chug-alugging his coffee, going to take a whiz (not bothering to wash his hands)—then he leans over the tub, grabs this stiff-bristled brush of his, takes another breath (the water *still* plenty hot, mind you), commences to scrub everything that comes into his hand, and dumps it willy-nilly into the rinse. When the rinse tub is brimming full, he reaches in—lifting and roughing the dishes together into manageable stacks—then lays these rough stacks on the drainboard beyond the glassware and mugs (now mostly drain-dry), stacking the dishes like the well-sliced loaves of bread. He loads more dishes into the wash-tub, dries his hands, and before the drying dishes can drain onto the glassware, he delivers the glasses and mugs to the front of the kitchen near the water cooler and the Pyrex coffee maker. Then he washes the next tub of dishes. When this first round of drainboard dishes is dry, he flips the stacks together and delivers them to the front—the special platters on the shelf above the griddle, the bowls next to the steam table, where the soup pot simmers on the back burner—everything a-clatter. When this whole first round of dishes is done (some still soaking in the rinse tub, some drying), Paco stoops under the sink and pulls out that laundry washtub of well-soaked flatware. He takes handfuls of knives and forks and spoons and dribbles them into the bleach rinse, sometimes scrubbing this piece or that piece specially. When the flatware is well rinsed, he spreads it out on the drainboard rubber mesh so it won't get spotted with rust. (When the county inspector is coming, he always calls a day ahead. Paco will scrub each piece of flatware with kitchen cleanser and a Brillo pad, soak them in a nauseating, extra-heavy solution of bleach rinse, and dry everything spotlessly with a clean linen towel—the hand drying exactly contrary to what the county says is sanitary and healthful, but the inspector will give a citation to any work less thorough.) And when the knives and forks and spoons are dry, he scoops them up by the handfuls and stows them in the gray rubber bins under the counter, where Ernest can easily dip in and get a table setting.

When the glassware and dishes and flatware are finished, Paco does the first of the cook pots and pans, the baking sheets and skewers, the casserole dishes and roasting pans. When he's finished with those, the bus pans are full again, so Paco stows the cooking gear and makes another round of the dining room, but first he drains the tubs, scours them out, and refills them (again with the hottest water he can stand). And amid all this are the endless interruptions: calls for more coffee mugs, spoons, special platters, the purveyors arriving—the bread man, the butcher, the linen man, the dairy man. They all come at different times, and each time Paco has to drop what he's doing and help unload.

And somewhere in here Paco gets his own breakfast, takes another whiz, refills coffee mugs, refills napkin dispensers, clears away more dishes—helping out in the dining room—fetches supplies for Ernest from the walk-in freezer.

The process is straightforward and mechanical, James, all arms and back, side-stepping and skipping—Paco leaning over the washtub, slopping garbage and burning-hot soapy bleach water on his T-shirt and trousers and doubled-up apron; his fingernails are white with grease and his face squinched up and one eye squeezed shut because of the cigarette he keeps in his lips. First the breakfast dishes (often every dish in the place) and some of the pots and pans, then the lunch rush and the rest of the pots and pans, then catch up all afternoon (Paco coming to know many of the dishes and much of the cookware as individual objects—on sight; knowing that he washes some things five and six times a day). At noon Ernest turns on the AM radio for the commodity prices—the farmers eating lunch listen especially closely—(". . . September wheat up a half, 300 cattle down 32 cents, 150 sheep up a quarter to a half, December-delivered soy beans steady to a dime higher . . .") and the weather ("It'll be a lingering high pressure through Thursday, ladies and gentlemen, then good news, rain for sure. Humid through the weekend and more rain . . ."), and rock and roll music ("Wild, wild horses couldn't drag me away," the Rolling Stones croon—Paco imagining them leaning back and screaming—"*Wild, wild* horses . . ."). Some afternoons Paco gets to sit down for his lunch—a half-pound hamburger on black bread with all the trimmings (Paco just plain helps himself, James) and a quart milkshake, then a quick smoke out back (taking the garbage with him when he goes), more Boston coffee with plenty of sugar, and back to work.

By eight o'clock Paco's back is plenty warm with pain and sore as hell, his legs ache and his face tingles, and he's ready for his medication.

And late in the evening, after dark, Big Buddy (the county forest preserve cop—a guy bigger than Russell) and Officers Miller and Webb (the two night-shift town cops) come wandering in, casual and assertive, mooching their dinners. Ernest always obliges them. ("Might as well, we'd be throwing the food out otherwise!" he'd tell you, James—"Cops are cops anywhere and everywhere, young man. Don't never not feed cops.") Big Buddy leaves his squad car in front of the door (where the whole town can't help but see it), comes in, his holster squeaking, throws a leg over one of the middle stools as well as he is able, and slaps his hands on the counter—dap, dappity-dap-dap, dap-dap:

> *Open the door, Henry,*
> *And let me in!*

Then he says to Paco, busy at the back, "Well, *Slug*, what's good that's new!" To which Paco always looks up and answers, "Officer Walsh, don't call me Slug." And a little later, when Miller and Webb come in, they're always decked out fit to kill, James—blue uniforms with stitched-in creases, red piping, silver whistles and name tags, special shoulder patches, fancy belts with their revolver ammunition, Mace cans, handcuffs, and whatnot. And some nights they sit there for the longest time, eating and gossiping.

After closing Paco finishes up the last of the dishes, cleans the tables and chairs, stools, and countertops, dry-wipes the blower hood over the griddle and the steam table, takes out the last of the garbage, and dry-mops the dining-room floor. Every Saturday night Paco also scrubs the stove and the walk-in freezer, and cleans out the grease trap under the washtubs—the trap about the size of a shoebox. He unhooks the top, then lifts out the screen and scrapes that foul, gray viscous mush into the garbage. And, James, cleaning the grease trap never fails to remind Paco of that day and a half he spent by himself at Fire Base Harriette—it is the stink, the stench of many well-rotted human corpses—and always sends him home Saturdays looking for a drink, "Just the whiskey, thanks. Skip the ice," he'll say to Myrna at the Geronimo Hotel.

While we're on the subject of work, James, it's as true a fact as there is that when Alpha Company—us grunts—would hump back to our base camp at Phuc Luc for a couple days' rest (stand-down, we called it), Lieutenant Stennett got so he didn't much care what we did just so long as "every swinging dick" made morning roll call. We never much told him, and Stennett—finally smarting up—never much asked. Some of us would sneak off to Tu Duc Phuc's #1 Souvenirs and Car Wash in town and get laid. Some of us would dawdle around the company nursing our diarrhea, bored out of our fucking skulls and homesick to boot, drinking anything we could get the top off of, writing letters home and playing penny-ante poker. The walking wounded among us would gobble our Darvons and antibiotics, resting up as best we could for the next move-out.

But Paco and Gallagher and Jonesy and Jigs, the medic, and some of the rest of us, would troop down to bunker number 7 on the east perimeter—that bunker, James, about chest-high and as big as a two-car garage—where we could sit and drink our beer and smoke our dope, shooting the shit, in peace. We would smear that foul-smelling insect repellent on ourselves, and still we would swat mosquitoes all night. It was a constant motion of heads and hands, James, quietly slapping at them or brushing them away, or mildly scratching. Jigs would bring the makings for the jays and a three-legged stool he snitched from the medics' hooch. Paco would bring this shit-for-nothing lawn chair, and would sit so deeply in it, with his knees way up, that he looked as though he were sitting in a barrel. Gallagher would sit on a wooden ammo crate as if it were the bottom step of a porch stoop back on the block, and would lean against the bunker and let the cool of it soak into his back—those sandbags fucked up with mortar hits and near-misses. And Jonesy would sit directly above him on the edge of the shallow-slanted roof, with his legs dangling over and his back to the rolls of concertina wire, and the marsh bubbling with slime and the beat-to-hell woodline a hundred meters opposite. Jonesy had to crouch almost double because we talked in hissing whispers.

If you stood back from those two, James, you'd swear that Gallagher and Jonesy looked like a totem—lots of guys said that: Jonesy's ashy, caramel-colored skin, pink nails, and bright black eyes, astonishing eyes; the livid scar along his jaw and under his lips; the lumpy razor rash; the well-oiled 12-gauge shotgun laid across his lap, and a pair of blacked-up, well-tended jungle boots ("Man's got to have some prideful fuckin' feelin' about some goddamn thing," he'd tell you). And literally between Jonesy's knees would be Gallagher's stubby face and pug ears, his bull neck and short thick fingers ("Golden Gloves motherfucker," we'd tease him, and laugh; "Fuck *you* up, boy," he'd tease right back, and grin, knocking his knuckles together, his eyes twinkling). He wore a green towel draped around his neck and his .357 Magnum packed in his shoulder holster, his feet flat on the ground, and that Bangkok R & R red-and-black dragon tattoo on his forearm from his wrist to his elbow shining like a trophy in the moonlight ("Got this here in a tattoo parlor," he'd say, bragging his head off, "that was part opium den, part fag whorehouse. That old papa-san must've had *thousands*, and I picked through them and finally took this sucker. It's a honey," he'd say, showing it around).

One night Gallagher had a bottle of Johnnie Walker Red. "Me and my man Paco scrounged this here bottle of John Dub-ya," and Gallagher shook the bottle in all our faces, "scrounged it from that goddamned Goody Two-shoes Captain Culpepper." Gallagher jerked his head up the hill toward Culpepper's tent—the captain's silhouette stooped over his famous Scrabble game—"Letting *him* drink this shit, why you might as well knock the neck off with a claw hammer and pour every last fucking drop down that Bravo Company piss tube across the way there!" Gallagher pointed over at the Bravo Company tents, then waved his hand in front of his face, making a pass or two at the mosquitoes. He cracked the seal, took a healthy swig—it *was* his bottle, James—and passed it on. (As the night wore on, the bottle emptied sip by sip, and you could hear it slosh more and more; the ring of it more and more mellow.)

Paco passed out the beers, and Jonesy and Jigs made the jays and passed them out. Then we sat quiet and absorbed in that small circle for the longest time, drinking and smoking—ruminating.

Gallagher slouched back against the bunker more and more, grumbling and muttering. If you listened close you could hear him repeating, "Shit. Fucking shit," growling with a deep, sharp voice. A couple days before, a Bravo Company man got his arm shattered in a mortar barrage, and it was this incident that Gallagher brooded over. Gallagher had seen it happen by the oddest chance, but it was not the actual event he picked over—the man's arm the last piece of anatomy pulled into the bunker, that 6o-mm round hitting right near with a hard *crack* the way they always ripped, leaving a crater that wasn't much more than a boot scuff. No, Gallagher wasn't thinking about that—"Seen that plenty, Jack!"—but rather, the funny, dumbshit look that came over the guy's face when he raised himself up and took a good long look down where the stump of his arm was—just below the elbow—as shaggy as a buckskin fringe. Or, as Gallagher later told Lieutenant Stennett, "Just the same as you'd shove a rolled-up newspaper into the business end of a roaring room fan, *sir*," looking right at Stennett as though it was he that done it.

Paco watched Gallagher slurp foam from his beer and stare at the smooth impression the whiskey bottle made in the pillowy, dusty dirt between his feet. Gallagher was mulling all that over, Paco knew, but then suddenly he shivered all over like a horse chasing flies and changed the subject on himself. He whipped out a cigar (he was smoking Antonio Y Cleopatra then) and lit it with his famous "Fuck you up, boy" Zippo lighter—the cigar tip soon cherry red and his head enveloped in billowing smoke; the air still, the smoke rising with ease and glowing strangely in the clear, undiminished moonlight.

(Almost everyone in the company had a PX Zippo lighter, James, and many of us had it inscribed with that parody of the Fourth verse of the Twenty-third Psalm:

> *Yea, though I walk through the valley*
> *of the shadow of death, I will fear no*
> *evil: for I am the meanest mother*
> *fucker in the valley.*

But Gallagher—the company killer, the company clown, a man both simple and blunt—had his Zippo engraved with his all-purpose response:

> *Gonna fuck*
> *you up,*
> *boy.*)

Gallagher looked at Paco as though the two of them shared a secret, and said, "I think about my old man sometimes. You?" And Paco, whose father was long dead, said, "Yeah." Gallagher swigged at the whiskey as it came around and cleared his throat with a growl. There was no melancholy in his voice, same as the night he told us about one of his older brothers killed in a car crash—*raining* like hell, *sideswiped* an abutment.

"My father drove a Chicago city bus—Chicago Motor Coach, CTA; drove streets like long Western and Lincoln, Kedzie-Kimball-California and Lunt-Touhy, Broadway and Sheridan Road. And I remember he used to come home nights ass-whipped tired, just *draggin'* his ass. My brothers and my ma and me would be sitting at the dinner table and we'd hear him and his goddamned galoshes coming up the front porch steps, and then he'd burst in the front door. We'd all look over our shoulders and see him in this big mirror that hung over the davenport in the living room. The copper weather stripping on the door would always twang—Ma kept it that way so that no matter how easy you tried to sneak it open it would always twang (it'd make your eyeballs just squeak); there'd be no comin's or goin's in her house *she* didn't know about. It'd be the dead of fucking winter, see, so he'd be wearing his huge, heavy coat with the stiff, thick collar, something like those big lumbering pea-coat-looking things that railroad men used to wear—only with more pockets and *much* heavier—and a pair of ordinary garden gloves. I tell you aside, I don't think my old man had a decent pair of gloves his whole fucking life.

"Everyone else went back to dinner, but I always watched him undress. First he'd pull off those gloves, one finger at a time, and lay them palm up on this squatty radiator we had by the front door. By springtime the fingers would curl into claw-looking things, and the cotton would fray at the fingers and they would unravel to the knuckles. Next'd come this gray scarf my great-aunt got him one year, that thing looped around his neck and tied like an ascot. Then he'd do the coat buttons—big as silver dollars, they were—and haul that coat off and hang it, and the scarf, on a side hook at the back of the closet. A big brass thing you could hang a side of beef on. Then he had two sweaters—one a thick, loose, golfer-looking thing, and underneath *that* was a close-knit, navy-blue V-neck he'd had since God-knows-when and had patches and darned places aplenty. And all that while he'd be standing there in these big-ass, ugly, fucking galoshes—big as coal hods—unbuckled but with his thick serge trousers shoved down into them, real sloppy. He'd pry those fuckers off, and if it'd snowed or rained, there'd be melted snow or mud sprayed all over Ma's prized paint job. The galoshes went on this big baking sheet behind the door.

"Well, then he'd start with his bus-driver gear—punch and changer and watch—and the big leather belt they hung on. That fuckin' changer was as big as the cast-iron bulldog that held open the kitchen door. There was a penny slot, two slots for nickels, one slot for dimes, a couple slots for quarters, and one slot for halves. I'd guess thirty-five, forty dollars. There was a slot for silver dollars, but he never used it. Bad luck, somehow, he told me once. Then would come the punch he had in a leather holster engraved with his initials—DDG—and kept clipped to the belt. The punch was real hefty, German-made, and would give you a star-shaped hole. He set the changer and punch on Ma's gateleg table, which was all ruined with gouges and scratches, and gray with water spots. Then he'd pull his pocket watch from the shirt pocket where he kept his pencils—that watch as big as your hand, 17 jewels, with Roman numerals and a sweep second hand as thin as a sewing needle. He put that down with the changer and punch. I remember, too," Gallagher said, snorting and grinning, "he used to pull that fuckin' thing out at Thanksgiving and Christmas, and bullshit my uncles that it cost him a month's pay and took food out of our mouths. He had it on a braided leather fob about as long as your arm, which drooped into his lap when he was driving, and he had a habit of running that fob through his fingers, stroking it—the same as you see old women working their rosaries at church—ticking off the stitches. He laid down the watch with the changer and punch, coiling the fob around it like a Sunday sailor coiling a deck rope." And Gallagher coiled that fob in the air so we could all see it, as dark as it was.

Gallagher poured some of the whiskey in his beer, stirring it around a time or two, and took a slug. "Then he'd haul off that belt of his, and I tell you, Jack, you could hear that fuckin' thing snap through every loop. You sure could tell what kind of an evenin' it was going to be by the sound of that fuckin' belt. If anyone was counting on a lickin' that night, you could see him flinch but good. My old man would coil that sucker around his fist, set it down on the gateleg, and drape the buckle end of it over the coin slots of the changer. I swear to God, Jack, he could count money by the look of the stack it made, by the heft of a handful of it. So may God pity the poor fuckin' fool who snitched as much as a dime, he would know. I remember many a night going up to bed and looking down around behind at the bottom of those stairs and that gateleg, and there'd be that fuckin' changer, chockful of coins, with the buckle end of that wide fuckin' belt laid over it just as easy and casual as you'd put your hand on somebody's shoulder from behind. That was the belt we got our lickin's with, you understand? I re-member many a night curled up as tight as a fist under my covers, listening to one or another of my brothers getting a whipping—them hopping around downstairs on all fours like a damn crab—my old man stompin' after them, shoving furni-ture aside and thrashing at them with that fuckin' belt—bellowing, *screaming* angry. Shit, bub! You could stuff a blanket and an afghan and a pillow apiece into your ears and you could *still* hear that goddamned belt rip and whistle through the air. My brothers and me got scars from that fuckin' buckle, which was one of those ordinary, square-looking, nickel-silver affairs with a thick crossbar.

"Anyway," Gallagher said, taking a moment to draw on his cigar and blow smoke rings up into the still night air, "my old man would stand in front of that closet—'putting away his work,' he called it. Some nights he'd come right in to dinner and some nights he'd go straight upstairs, but some nights he would stagger into the living room and slump into his easy chair. He'd crouch nearly double, his head in his hands, half blinded by headaches, squeezing his scalp for all he was worth, with those cold, rawed-up fingers of his, and his eyes'd be red and milky, shining—and sometimes those fuckin' headaches went on all night; years later he told me he could feel his face droop like a gob of warmed wax.

"My ma and my brothers and me'd sit around that table, looking at him, and I'd look the longest—me being the youngest had something to do with that, I expect. And every once in a while he'd stand there in front of that closet for a *long* time —that closet where everything hung, don't you see: football gear and mechanic's tools, Monopoly and croquet, the flashlights and *Reader's Digest* and Lionel trains, the coats and boots and shopping bags. He'd stand there in those galoshes and that big heavy coat of his, stinking of fuel oil and diesel fumes, and this look of pale and exhausted astonishment would come over him, like he just woke up and couldn't bring himself to believe where he was and what he was looking at.

"Fuckin'-A," Gallagher said, disgusted ("Goddamned drunk," as Jonesy would say). "My old man busted his ass all his life, and all's he got out of it was beat-up hands, bad eyes, and a bend in his back.

"And you know what else," Gallagher said, sniffing and laughing at the discovered irony, then taking another heavy swig of his boilermaker. "That was the same look as come over the poor fuckin' fool from Bravo Company a couple days ago when he drew himself out of that bunker and took a good long look at what was left of his arm. Then the pain worked itself up his arm and into his face, and after that he never stopped screaming." And we all had to shiver then, remembering the screams.

"Fuckin' Bravo Company," Gallagher said, brushing at the mosquitoes in his hair and sitting up—as good as done with that bottle of whiskey—"How you gonna have any pity on those geeks?"

One night after closing, Ernest locks the doors and turns out most of the lights, brings up a cider jug of his sweet, home-made rosé from the basement, pulls up one of those big potato-chip cans into the middle of the dining room, pours himself an 8-ounce juice tumbler of wine, and drinks about half of it down. Ernest is a Guadalcanal Marine who went ashore at Iwo Jima with Chandler Johnson's battalion and climbed Mount Suri-bachi.

He sits in the middle of the dining room with his back to his collection of wall clocks—old Regulator time-punch clocks and railroad clocks, cheap sunburst quartz clocks, clocks with vegetables for numerals, a grinning kitty-cat kitchen clock with ticking tail, and everything in between.

Suddenly he blurts out, "You wounded in Vietnam, eh?" —Paco having become a curiosity since he came to work in the Texas Lunch; Paco hustling trays of dishes, his cane hang-ing on a nail set to swinging as he goes by, all those scars up and down his arms.

Paco says, "Yeah," from the back of the kitchen, straight-ening up from his stoop, stopping work for an instant, "Vietnam. Sure as shit." His hands drip soap and the dishes clatter beneath him.

"*I* was wounded on Guadalcanal *and* Iwo Jima," Ernest says. "I guess that about makes me a fucking patriot, but I'll be fucked if you'll see me fly the flag. Not Flag Day or the Fourth of July. Not Memorial Day or Veterans Day—which *used* to be called Armistice Day, see?—no kind of goddamned day. And I don't fly it right side up, upside down, inside out, crosswise, ass backward, or fuck-you otherwise."

He sits on his potato-chip can, pours himself another juice glass of sweet rosé wine, and we can see the rose tattoo about the size of a baseball on the fat part of his arm, James. "Got this here *tattoo*," he says, shouting so Paco will hear and know what he's talking about, "in New Zealand, and let me tell you, young man, New Zealand *pussy*, now there was some *grateful* women. *Fuck* anything that would stand still. Even the company shitsack got his ashes hauled while we were there.

"On Guadalcanal there was this big-headed Jap stood up on this ridge we had been fighting over for a week and more. One company fucked up but good and another about chewed half to death—everybody else sick as a goddamned dog. We're hunkered down in these shitty trenches, when this guy stands up in his rags, some NCO-looking cat, with an officer's pistol in one hand and this here sword in the other." And Ernest whips out a sword about the size of a good carving knife in a stiff leather sheath decorated with a well-faded tassel. "That guy—some Imperial fucking Marine—stands there holding this shit way up, semaphore-fashion, like he was showing it to every guy on that whole fucking island, and the harbor, too, for that matter. Then he gives a yell, screams his face red, and this kid from Omaha down the line reaches his M–1 up to diddle the guy, but we said, 'Hold on there, young man, this may get interesting.' That big-headed Jap quivers, and stamps his feet, holding the scabbard—it was bright green back then, grass-green—then he put that pistol upside his head, working it back and forth like he's screwing it into his skull, and then when he's sure everyone is watching him—some guys shouting encouragement, 'Go ahead, you sorry hunk of shit, blow your brains out! Slit your fucking throat, you ugly, slant-eyed prick!' —he squeezes off a round, jacks his head to the side, and drops dead all in one motion. Everyone understood sure enough that he was the last one up there, so before the lieutenant could say the first word, we all jump up and run, scrambling up that ridge which was as steep as an old house roof. I dived for the sword, and this is it. I got his leggings, too, but I traded those the day after for a bottle of swipe" (back-yard booze made from canned fruit, James).

"Iwo Jima was this bullshit little island, see," and Ernest looks around behind him out the doorway, as if that island were a spot of tar in the street, "out in the middle of no fucking place. The Japanese were dug in all over that son-of-a-bitch, like it was a fortified sponge. And you could pert near stand on Suribachi at one end of the island and piss off the other end," he says, sipping steadily from his wine and getting carried away. "About all I remember is the fucking smell—of which there was plenty, you understand? Sulphur sand. Gunpowder smoke. Greasy sweat. Diesel fumes. Tons, it must have been *tons* of shit—human and otherwise—there were four Marine divisions and more than 20,000 Japanese, see, everybody eating and shitting. And we were dying like flies. The Japs were dying like flies—there were fucking corpses sticking up out of the dirt and everywhere. All we found of one guy was an arm's length of his gut laid out on the road between wheel ruts out in the middle of nowhere, as if it'd been bounced off the back of somebody's truck. The day we put up the flag—it wasn't me, but I was near there—why, everybody on that island stopped to watch. All those ships cruising or moored fast or hustling supplies ashore—thousands of sailors —stopped to watch. Everybody felt that all the fucking work was worth something, though the fighting went on for three more weeks. Couple of years ago I was traveling through Washington, D.C., on my way to my sister's in Virginia Beach, and happened to drive near that Iwo Jima statue that's over by the cemetery, and you could see it from clear across the river. Six guys breaking their balls, muscling that goddamned flag up— one guy reaching up real hard and it's just out of fingertip touch. Close only counts in horseshoes, I remember thinking to myself. Work's work, but I tell you from the bottom of my heart that Iwo Jima was a sloppy, bloody butt-fuck.

"I saw two guys get some wild hair up their asses and get Congressional Medals of Honor. Dumb-fuck, ballsy, sons-a-bitches. Crazy motherfuckers. Both killed stone dead," Ernest says. "I saw Chandler Johnson, the colonel himself, catch his lunch. He got a direct hit with a mortar round about the size of a 55-gallon drum, or one of them dumpsters. Fuck—meat all over everything. And by the time the smoke cleared, he was just one more dead guy, one more smell, one more hole in the ground.

"Well, one day—on Iwo, this was—a hunk of shrapnel blew through me like a railroad spike and ripped this other guy's arm clean off, right about the middle of the biceps. We had no bandages, no tourniquets, no fucking thing. The corpsman held the stump with his bare hands like you'd double up a garden hose—clamped off all the veins like that. I got this sucking chest wound"—and Ernest pulls up his T-shirt to reveal a purplish, crescent-shaped scar about the size of a lemon rind—"this fucking sucking chest wound that just wouldn't shut up." Ernest says now, plenty drunk. "After twenty-two days on that goddamned island, guys getting fucked up left and right, me scared shitless every minute of the time, I figured it was my turn to get dragged down to some aid station or other and die, bleeding to death, on some blood-ied-up litter. Some guy pulled me by the back of the shirt down this goddamned hill—don't s'pose you ever heard of the Meat Grinder?—and I heard the shirt ripping, thinking to myself, Ernest, this son-of-a-bitch is going to rip that fucking thing off your back and leave you for dead, and won't that be a fine pickle. Then I passed out. Woke up aboard some hospital ship, the *Solace* or the *Endure* or the *Behave-and-Get-Well* or some other bullshit name as that, strapped to a clean bunk, chest all bandaged up—those stitches really stung—the ship rolling back and forth in those easy, lazy, fine-weather swells," Ernest says, swinging that juice glass this way and that.

"Got to Yokohama right after the war, and there were Marines and sailors all over everything, like stink on shit. We'd prowl up and down the streets and little-bitty side alleys," Ernest says, holding up his thumb and first finger to signify "little-bitty," "looking for pussy; looking for Imperial Marines, the guys we fought on Guadalcanal. I was with this horny New York fella would fuck anything would lift its leg. Well, one day we caught this one poor cocksucker, took him into a hooch yard, and just about beat him to death. He'd been wear-ing his Imperial Marine uniform, tunic and knickers and leggings—think about it now, it was probably the only clothes he owned—but fuck it, man, plenty good Marines bellied up because of cocksuckers like him. Told him we see him wearing that fucking uniform one more time, we'd kill him plain and clean. 'Shoot you down like a dog, motherfucker,' that New York fella said. 'Chop your fucking nuts off and feed them to the squirrels, then chop your fucking head off and throw that son-of-a-bitch *a-way*'; everybody knows if you chopped their heads off, their souls couldn't join their fucking ancestors or some cornball bullshit like that—something to do with their religion. We told him the only thing that saved his worthless fucking asshole was the Hiroshima bomb.

"Sure was the only thing saved mine," Ernest says, and pours himself another big glass of rosé wine, and drinks it half down.

"One fine day this full-bird colonel pulled up in a deuce-and-a-half and volunteered a bunch of us, so we pile in his truck, and off we go south—past thatch-roofed villages and truck gardens and squiggly, terraced rice paddies, and folks that looked real ragged. We get to Hiroshima, where they had dropped that fucking bomb. And, man, there wasn't nothing left of that town worth bothering to piss on. I was on the Canal from start to finish. I was on Iwo for twenty-two fucking days, and I'll be dipped in shit but I've seen guys get their balls broke. Now, the Air Force had been fire-bombing the absolute piss out of Tokyo, but *this* was one bomb—one minute, one morning, one day in your life—*ker-ploosh*. Seventy thousand people just as decent as you and me—*poof*—all that was left of some was their shadow on a brick wall. See shit like that and your life is changed," Ernest says, easing back against the edge of a dining-room table, a wearisomeness coming over him in a single breath. "I may have hated them right down to their fucking eyeballs and buttonholes, but nobody deserves shit like that. Man, the kicker was that even the fucking rubble was worthless. At least in Germany—Dresden and Hamburg, places we firebombed the holy shit out of just for the fun of it, just so they could take pictures and show the fucking generals—they could sort out the rubble, pile it up, dust it off a little, and reuse it. But what dumb son-of-a-bitch do you know is going to use bricks—what bricks there were in Hiroshima—that glow in the dark? Looking down at them from the back of that truck—folks huddled around make-do camps and lean-to aid stations—you didn't know whether to laugh your ass off ('Fuck you! Fuck this whole godforsaken island!') or cry your eyes out; thinking about your own family and the town where *you* came from. I mean, they'd been feeding their kids to the green machine (is that what they call it?) and eating shit themselves for years. You wound up thinking to yourself, How much humiliation can ordinary people endure? We hung around some aid station, helping out, killing time and shooting the shit, then drove back to Yokohama. Three weeks after that I rotated. Seasick the whole trip back—sicker than a dog."

Paco stands in front of that rinky-dink back sink with his belt buckle hooked over the lip of the tub, scrubbing up the last of the dishes before he fetches the last of the pots and pans, and does the glasses and silverware, listening with automatic attention to Ernest's droning talk, with his apron drooping in his lap and that jug of wine shining in the little light of the dining room. Ernest talks on and on, swinging that juice glass this way and that, hoisting it in the air for salutes and toasts, and, when he's done talking, slumps back against a table for a moment, then clears out the cash register, counts up the till, and takes it to the night deposit at the bank.

Paco dips his arms ino the hot lye-soap wash water again and again, the work stinging. He remembers how Gallagher came back from his R & R with that red-and-black tattoo of a dragon on his forearm from his wrist to his elbow, a bunch of us standing in the yellowy light of dusk taking our showers under the wing-tank spigots. We soaped up, rinsed down, the young women KPs at the mess hall watching. Our pale legs and buttocks shining wet, like so many apples—the white guys tanned many shades of brown and the black guys many shades of ashy black. Gallagher couldn't help but brag his head off about what a good time he had. "That Thai pussy, now, that's some great pussy," he said, standing tall, letting a single stream of water pour over him, wiggling his toes. "This one gal had a cunt like a catcher's mitt. You could eat it till your jaws got tired. Fuck it till your pecker got as mushy as homemade Play-Doh. You could wrassle it, blubber your nose in it"—all of us standing around him, slapping at the water, laughing, splashing in the hard mud and sharp gravel underfoot— "fuck it frontways, fuck it backways, fuck it standing on your head; swing it high; swing it low-down—it made absolutely no difference to her, she squeaked and squealed just fine. Now, this here tattoo," he said, holding up his arm so everyone could see the thing, which became known in the company as Gallagher's Bangkok R & R red-and-black-dragon tattoo. "I about *died* when the guy put it on.

"When I first met the girl—Nanette, she said her name was—we're out strolling the boulevard and she asks me what is it that I want. And I say, without missing so much as half a step, that I want a good stiff drink, I want to get laid, and I want a tattoo. We get pints of whiskey and schnapps and take them back to my room, and have a couple glasses of very good booze, and then she takes off my clothes and her clothes and just about fucks my brains out, and my man, when she got through with me I did not know yonder from hither." Gallagher took a moment to point at the mess hall on one hand and the woodline behind the marsh on the other. "Then after we'd napped some, she wakes me up in the middle of the night and says, 'Psst! Come with me.' She steps back into her raspberry-colored summer dress—it makes my balls roar just to think about her—and I get dressed and off we go. We tiptoe through the lobby, and walk through the intersection there. Up one street and down the other. Cross an open sewer. We turn. We go straight. We turn the other way. We stop at a sidewalk place for shrimp and bread and beers—it's the middle of the night, mind you, and there's still plenty of folks out and around—nice city, Bangkok. We hit a narrow side street and walk up it; you could reach out and touch houses and storefronts on both sides of the street—the place smelled like spicy-hot food and pussy and reefer. All of a sudden we duck into one place—middle of the night, mind—and there's a couple dozen old mama-sans sitting around on plain benches, stitching shirts with needle and thread. When we come in they rise and bow. We climb these rickety stairs. Go down a hallway, wooden louvered doors on either side. *Man*-oh-man, I just fucking know I'm gonna get jackrolled! I got half my roll in a money belt tied around my waist. We come to a door at the end of the hall, open it, and we're outside. We walk along this catwalk-looking thing nailed to the wall with galvanized roofing nails, and it shimmies. *Shit!* We jump a roof

—her sandals clacking—and walk along the ridge of it, along those terra-cotta tiles—me thinking, Man, they're never gonna find my fucking body—the street glowing below us. I remember looking out and seeing couples, GIs and whores, strolling along the pavement, but looking like they're walking in the air, floating along. The street the same color as the sky, but I'm still about half-stumbling drunk, so I figure I could have been seeing anything. We jump onto a high gallery. Pass windows where some old Airedale-looking bitch is suckling a litter of pups; an old woman with witchy hair sits on the edge of a huge black-lacquered bed with her head in her hands, crying real hard. Regular-looking folks fucking on one thing or another."

"Ordinary, round-eyed white folks," as Jonesy would say, "looking for kicks"—they don't call it Bangkok for nothing, James.

"Guys in dago T-shirts sitting around their little-bitty kitchen, smoking this and that. Finally we get to this one window, with bullshit-red plastic drapes blowing in and out," Gallagher says.

"We have arrived at the tattoo parlor. Little did I know. The old guy who runs the place is God knows how old, smoking some foul kind of dope that he's rolled into a joint about the size of a jumbo crayon. Well, he sits me down in one of those antique, hand-crank, French barber chairs, and he jaws and palavers some, and starts showing me tattoos up one side of his arm and down the other. Big red heart with dagger stuck through it. A cartoon devil with horns and a forked tail, and the mother is holding a limp scroll that reads, 'Little shit.' Fancy nameplates—'For the girl of your dreams.' Nanette said, sitting on a sewing machine, swinging her legs. I'm sitting in this bullshit chair, beginning to pour sweat and sober down a little, and I tell the guy I don't want no chickenshit Marine Corps crapola. 'What else you got and make it snappy, papa-san.' Well, sir," said Gallagher, spreading around, loud, start-ing to laugh at his own fun, "he goes into the next room and brings back four or five queer-looking fags who've been sitting in a parlor-looking room drinking some freaky, smelly booze and turning tricks. These guys swish on in the room and stand there la-di-da, sparkle-eyed and funny teeth and grin-ning like apes. The old man had them pull open their robes, and there it was, Jack, every tattoo in the world: monsters, flowers, mazes, portraits, machines, churchy tableaux, dream scenes—this one fag had green-and-gray gilt embroidered around his crotch—can you imagine a Bangkok fag whore-house that caters to guys with a tattoo fetish? I pull out a cigar and tell the guy, 'Naw, get these fags outta here. What the fuck you think I am?' And the old guy's getting pissed. He pulls out a beer bottle box with stacks of what look like glass negative photographic plates. Old. Pictures of more guys. Somebody's big, broad back with a full-rigged clipper, under sail and leaning plenty to leeward. Another guy with the Taj Mahal. Another one had a Harley-Davidson Indian motorcycle —kickstand and all. Another had the regimental portrait of some Pakistanis with knickers and shorts, turbans and those big-ass Enfield rifles and cartridge belts hung all over them— it was just as clear as a newspaper photograph. The old guy's showing me his antiques, and when I keep shaking my head, he gets this look on his face, like I just pissed on his gera-niums. Then he whips out this photograph of this barrel-chested guy, stripped to the waist, with a big, scrubby mus-tache and his hair knotted up at the back of his head; he's got one fist on his hip, and's holding out his other arm, fisted to get his muscles solid, and there's this dragon—the grin, the nasty tail, the claw nails, the pig snout and curled-round scaly neck. 'That's it,' I say. 'I'll take *it*,' I say, and sit back, showing him on my arm where I want it. The old man starts right in while Nanette gets me a big glass of whiskey. Well . . ."

And Paco finished up the last of the deep baking pans—tomorrow's special will be turkey loaf with stewed tomatoes—remembering how Gallagher had short thick arms and how the red-and-black tattoo of that dragon twisted and twined up and down his forearm; how when Gallagher showed it he always made a big fist and would roll his wrist. Later that night, when Paco leans back into his pillows, luxuriating in the stupefying doses of Librium and Valium, he recalls the fascination all of us had with Gallagher's red-and-black, blue-and-green tattoo.

It may come as something of a surprise, James, but Paco, for all his trouble, has never asked, Why me?—the dumbest, dipstick question only the most ignorant fucking new guy would ever bother to ask.

Why *you*? Don't you know? It's your turn, Jack!

Not in all the hours that he lay terrifically wounded—the rest of us long gone, Paco as good as left for dead—did he ask. Not on that dust-off chopper with the medics delicately and expertly plucking debris from his wounds, Paco bursting with gratitude, whimpering and shivering from the cold. And not on any of these nights lately, after work, when Paco would sit up in bed, sore and exhausted, gazing down at himself—bitterly confronted with that mosaic of scars—waiting for his nightly doses of Librium and Valium to overwhelm him (like a showering torrent of sparks, some nights, or an avalanche of fluffy, suffocating feathers).

No, James, Paco has never asked, *Why me*? It is we— the ghosts, the dead—who ask, Why him?

So Paco is made to dream and remember, and we make it happen in this way, particularly on those nights when his work—washing the last of the dishes, clearing up and stowing down after closing—goes particularly well with no one to pester him, and he settles into a work rhythm, a trance almost ("I wash and God dries," he'll tell you, James). Even the burgeoning pain in his legs and back—that permanent aggravating condition of his life—blossoms and swells, warming him like a good steady fire of bottom coals. It is at those moments that he is least wary, most receptive and dreamy. So we bestir and descend. We hover around him like an aura, and declare (some of the townsmen have bragged and sworn they have seen us). Paco would finish his work virtually in the dark; Ernest, the boss, long gone to deposit the day's receipts; Paco turning around in his astonished pleasure at discovering the work so agreeable—entranced by the surprising ease of it— reaching around, dipping his hand into the last of the greasy bus pans for the next thing to soak and scrub and rinse clean. But everything is done, and dry; and his work is ended.

He would slip off his apron, soaking wet and sour with sweat, and hang it on a nail, straighten his T-shirt, take up his black hickory cane, and take that droning, warm feeling for the work out the back door and across the street to the Geronimo Hotel, up to his dingy little room overlooking the brick railroad alley at the back of Earl and Myrna's Bar downstairs.

He would flop headlong across the bed, with the sore pain of his wounds itching like the burning sting of a good hard slap.

It is at that moment we would slither and sneak, shouldering our way up behind the headboard, emerging like a newborn—head turned and chin tucked, covered head to toe with a slick gray ointment, powdery and moist, like the yolk of a hard-boiled egg, and smelling of petroleum. We come to stand behind him against the wall—we ghosts—as flat and pale as a night-light, easy on the eyes. We reach out as one man and begin to massage the top of his head; his scalp cringes and tingles. We work our way down the warm curve of his neck—so soothing and slack—and apply ourselves most deeply to the solid meat back of his shoulders. And Paco always obliges us; he uncoils and stretches out even more, and eases into our massage bit by bit, leaning into our invigorating touch wholeheartedly. And when Paco is most beguiled, most rested and trusting, at that moment of most luxurious rest, when Paco is all but asleep, *that* is the moment we whisper in his ear, and give him something to think about—a dream or a reverie.

Some nights he dreams escape dreams: being chased, sweating and breathless, into a large and spacious warehouse with a paving-stone floor crisscrossed with narrow ore-cart tracks (like trolley tracks, say), enormous whitewashed skylights overhead, and dusty cobwebs hanging down as thick as Spanish moss. There are huge cranes aloft, bolted fast to the thick cedar rafters, and long, greasy loops of winch chain hanging nearly to the floor. There is the echo-ous ring of Paco's every footfall, and water from burst pipes in distant rooms dripping into shallow puddles. Wandering from room to room, soon enough Paco hears trucks pulling up outside, the rattling of tailgate chains and the solid slamming of many doors. Paco moves on, compelled, and comes to a part of the building that opens out like a cathedral gallery, as spacious as a dirigible hangar (fine and airy). Flimsy ropes as light as felt hang down from the high cross timbers in clusters, like the creosoted ticking plumbers use to pack soil pipe joints with, as sour and overpowering as a bitter narcotic. And never far behind Paco is the grumbling of many voices, the heavy click of many boots, the hard tapping of many ax handles on the rough floor or the pipes that festoon the walls. There always comes a moment when Paco knows that in another instant they will turn the corner, come through a fire-door entrance, and be upon him (Paco twitching in his sleep, his heart pounding), as mad and murderous as a lynch mob. So he reaches up and gathers an armful of those ropes into a loose bundle, like a bouquet, and begins to shinny up—those ropes moist and as hairy as cat fur. And it is *always* slow going, James, an excruciating, dream-speed slow motion. He presses the clinging, goosy ropes so tightly that juice runs down his arms—oily as milkweed fuzz. He pulls himself up, curling his legs and feet around the bundle, then peels away his fingers and hands and arms, freeing himself with prodigious effort, then stretches his whole body upward with a sweeping, calculated lunge, gathering more ropes into a cable and hoisting himself up the next little bit. The higher he climbs, the more suffocating and stuffy is that creosote smell—as pungent as temple incense. By the time he has climbed up among the lowest rafters and narrow, spindly catwalks (with the milky skylights just beyond), Paco is nauseated and pouring sweat, his skin itching like crazy and as sticky as pine tar. But as hard and fast as he climbs, never in the dream does he escape, climbing through the veils of cobwebs and free of the ropes to clamber along the catwalks, and then up and out the open skylight. And always, James, those truckloads of men come to stand beneath him, switching those ax handles against their thighs, muttering and bitching.

Or he dreams of waiting rooms—the passenger lounge of a ferry boat, say: the solid iron floor deeply rumbling with the surging effort of the diesels and propeller screws, aft. The heavy furniture, long couches and wide easy chairs, slides this way and that as the boat rolls and scuds along in the heavy chop, shuddering. The boat makes its way through the contrary currents between high, rugged cliffs of a deep fjord (whitewashed with streaks of guano as thick as candle drippings), and many of the older passengers are plainly ill and troubled. Paco swings around the room, hanging on to the pillars (wrapped in varnished cord) to steady himself while he passes the hat (feeling sheepish and cheap, James), panhandling. "How 'bout it now. How 'bout a bit of change for old times' sake," he hears himself say, beseeching and apologetic at the same time, collecting the coins and bills in a collapsed wool watch cap. Outside, on the open-air deck, where the cars and campers are parked bumper to bumper, stem to stern, flocks of sea gulls soar and hover overhead, like a cloud of gnats, screaming and beckoning. Some of the passengers, desperate for entertainment, fetch loaves of bread and fling slices into the air—Frisbee-fashion—and the gulls dive down, crowing, to nip the slices in midair and then fight for scraps on the wing among themselves, swooping and dodging. And never does so much as a crumb touch the water; there are that many gulls and they are that good at the game. And in the dream, James, Paco always winds up with drooping pocketfuls of change—the money so solid in his pocket he can hardly drive his fingers through it—pressing his face against the cold porthole glass, staring forward, trying to impel the boat onward by the keenness and concentration of his gaze.

And some nights he dreams execution dreams. A group of soldiers, Paco among them, is led down a narrow, well-lit corridor—the hot-water piping overhead plenty warm, humming; the floors painted battleship gray, glistening with wax. The men are escorted into a small room of bare concrete, as crowded as a rush-hour elevator, everyone stuffy, hot and itchy. The group consists of one man from each platoon in three battalions of infantry—chosen by lot, volunteered—to be executed as punishment for some crime never mentioned. Cowardice? Mutiny? A fragging? The men stand bound with leather thongs twisted and looped around their necks and knotted severely around their wrists in back—as if this might be a way-station rest stop on the Bataan Death March, say (as tightly packed as if that basement vault were a death-camp-bound box car—so that if you fainted, James, you could not fall, and once you collapsed, you never came to). Some of the men are pale and woozy already in the claustrophobic air and extreme tension of anticipation. Some are as miserable-looking and stoic as if they're standing at ease, by company, on the Sunday-afternoon regimental drill field, waiting for a rainstorm to let up—"I just want to fucking sit down!" And some men are really pissed off—"I ain't done a goddamned thing, hear me!" Paco, at the back of the room, presses his forehead against the concrete—smelling of dust, with the raw imprint of the birch plywood grain as plain as day—the twisted thong around his neck lathered with sweat and nearly choking him. He can sense how very thick the wall is by how solid and profoundly cold is the concrete (a deep yellow, purple, and black—the colors of a deep bruise). That cold seeps into him, at first a pleasant comfort in that stuffy room, but then he becomes stiffly cold as the warmth is drawn from his body as neatly as a soundless whistle. Two plain-faced medics enter through the riveted steel door, dressed in long lab coats, one carrying a small medical case about the size of a first-aid kit spread open in both hands. The case contains a large glass-and-chrome syringe notched off in quarter inches, a set of five large needles, and one big bottle of bluish, pearlescent poison. The two medics efficiently muscle through the crowd, almost rowing with their shoulders. And when the executions begin, the medics stand on either side of a man; the first medic cuts the twisted-up thong with a jackknife, the man drops his arms—his sides relieved of the tension— sighing sharply as though enduring a burn. Then the medic takes up the hypodermic (the plunger with a large thumb ring), pinches a handful of flesh at the arm or the back of the neck, and stabs the needle in and squeezes the plunger home all in one neat motion. The executed man half gasps, as much from the surprise as from the sting of the needle, and sud- denly shivers as if he'd been plunged into a cold bath of cracked ice. In that same instant, the executed man rolls his eyes back into his head and droops to the floor. Paco leans against the concrete wall, feeling the sharp pain of the cold spreading through his body—the cold like a nail in his head where his skull touches it. Paco remembers (in the dream now, James) how the city dog pound used to kill its leftover dogs. Someone would hold the animal up by the loose skin at the neck, stretching the eyes, petting and stroking it, while someone else would jab the needle in—at the neck back of the ears—and inject the poison. (Not a breath later the dog would slump in the guy's arms. And if we stood at the door of the city pound loading dock, James, you'd see a pile of dogs, all shapes and sizes and colors, looking like so many ripped-up rugs, but with legs and ears and long black tongues.) The two medics execute first one man, then another, and another, stepping over the corpses. Sometimes they circle; sometimes they make a beeline; sometimes they move obliquely, like chess pieces; sometimes it's one right after another—a cluster fuck, we called it, James. Never in the dream do the executions cease, but never does the crowd thin—Paco standing, cramped, with the cold pouring into the back of his skull like dry-ice vapor spilling over a tabletop. Never do the medics change their flat, benign expressions—eyeing Paco out of the corners of their eyes—and never do they run out of fresh needles or does the bottle run dry of that pearlescent, metallic-tasting poison.

But just as often, James, Paco dreams of what it would have been like to leave Vietnam on his own two feet, the 2nd squad of the 2nd platoon humping along a flat orange road in full battle dress, bristling with guns and ammunition—radios, LAWS, claymores, frags, and all. We come to a large, glazed-brick building in the middle of a broad plain—a theater, say, or a gymnasium with sparkling brown windows that reflect everything darkly. Paco, urged always in the dream by a sudden, excited impulse, turns abruptly aside from us, calling, "Goodbye and take good care!" and we call back, "Take good care and fare thee well." He jumps a deep and narrow ditch, brimful with stagnant, brackish water and creamy with a bubbling scum. He sheds his rifle and bandoliers, his rucksack and flak jacket and pistol, as well as his gray gas-mask bag crammed with spools of black wire, his fillet knife, and other booby-trap makings. He walks on, peeling his T-shirt off his body, and into the thick pastel shade of many tall rubber trees. He jumps up the low steps of the building and comes right to the entrance, feeling that sliver of ice-cold air blowing through the split in the wide double doors—that steady blast burning as though he's being sliced in two. The door springs open, and in he goes, to a low, wide lobby of smooth gray carpet crowded with other homebound troops. A drooping banner at the far end of the lobby is festooned with red, white, and blue bunting, and reads:

WELCOME TO THE
451ST PROCESSING AND TRANSPORT
FACILITY (DET.)

CAPT. OMAR BERRY, CO

ALL INCOMING PERSONNEL
REPORT HERE

Paco makes his way among the tight, in-facing groups of soldiers—everyone decked out in their Class-A khakis, with their traveling gear piled in the middle of each group. Does Paco recognize any of the men?—everyone talking casually with their bulky greatcoats thrown over their arms, their collar brass glittering like 14k gold, their trouser creases as crisp and perfect as stitching; all of them standing tall and robust, faces full of color, healthy and soldierly. Paco—in the dream now, James—feels diminished, achy and rheumy with the sour nausea of heat exhaustion coming over him, his skin

much reddened, hot and dry to the touch. He finally makes it
through the doors under the welcome banner and into a broad
auditorium—the place sloping gently down like an Olympic
bleacher, but solid, and upholstered wall-to-wall with the
same gray carpet as the lobby. The place is always crammed
with more GIs—these decked out in sloppy, baggy fatigues—
and so crowded that you have to mind where you step. Men
sleep profoundly, curled up against their duffels and seabags,
sprawled across footlockers and boxes and other crated lug-
gage ready to ship. They use their shirts and field jackets for
pillows and lay their hands nonchalantly over souvenir rifles
—everything shipshape, registered, and tagged (French bolt-
action assault rifles, Chinese SKSs, and Russian AKs with
Chinese markings). Paco tiptoes exaggeratedly, like a ballet
clown, in his clumsy, filthy boots and baggy, rugged fatigues,
over the duffels and bundles and spread-out coats. And all the
while a smooth, well-modulated announcer's voice calls over
the public-address system an endless roster of names, ranks,
and parenthetical service numbers—like a recipe, James—
paging the men to be loaded aboard the charter planes that
wait outside on the tarmac, bound for home. There is a constant hubbub going on around Paco as he shoulders and urges
his way to the exit. But as many times as he has had the
dream, James, as many times as he has listened to that voice
(always the very air around the speakers throbbing and popping, *crackling* with static; Paco's flesh tingling), never can
he make out any of the names, and never does he hear his
own, "Paco Sullivan, US 54 800 409, step to the door . . ."

And the next morning Paco would always waken from
these dreams in the full, warm light of day with a start,
tangled in the sheets and turned every which way in bed.

And we, James—the dead, the ghosts who haunt him—long gone.

It is now the middle of a hot and muggy summer, and it has become Paco's habit to take a breather after the last of the dinner rush, before Ernest turns off the front lights and locks the doors.

Paco would take a pint jar of orange drink and a smoke and sit on the smooth concrete stoop in the full light of the doorway. The hard red rash of the lye soap on his arms would sting; the smoke rings he blows rise into the air, billowing; the sopping-wet linen apron would droop deeply in his lap. He would roll his shoulders and stretch, reaching around behind himself to drive his knuckles into his back, nodding and dipping his head this way and that. He'd smoke his Camels and guzzle his orange drink from the Mason jar, sitting on the top step of the stoop across the troughlike alley from Savic and Sons Hardware (the shadows in the stucco as peculiar as a moonscape), counting the iron bars on the high windows and listening for Ernest to padlock the front doors, pour himself a juice glass of rosé wine, splash some plain soda water on the griddle, and commence scraping up the day's grease and gunk with a putty knife.

Well, one night the lights in the front apartment of the Geronimo Hotel suddenly catch his eye. And Paco sees a young woman with fuzzy blond hair parading around in threadbare cotton underwear, bra and underpanties. The graying, dilapidated, sheer drapes puff into the room like banners—drawn by a large room fan at the back of the apartment, no doubt, James. Paco sits on that stoop in the alley with the cigarette smoke hot on the back of his hand, watching up at her that night and many another night; sometimes catching her traipsing around the room in a skimpy towel tucked into itself between her breasts—just out of the shower and whipping her hair around to help it dry (her hair as fine and light as collie puppy fur). And some nights she would have only her panties on, and she'd as good as show off, almost dancing, and Paco's cock would *stir* under his sour work pants—him catching long glimpses of her from one window to the next through the feathery droop of the sheers.

But one night he comes out earlier than usual and sits in his trancelike stupor in the deepest darkness beyond the doorway light next to the garbage dumpster. He stretches this way and that, listening to the pins and screws in his legs grating. The damp work pants pull at his knees; his wrinkly feet squish in his shoes. He has his juice jar and cigarette and a "strike anywhere" match, and glances up at the girl's windows (her name Cathy, James, student at the Wyandotte Teachers College west of town, and niece to Earl and Myrna). He sees her, dressed in that threadbare underwear of hers, pull up a chair near the window and sit deeply down, and stare into the back doorway of the Texas Lunch.

(For weeks now, James, Cathy would turn off all the lights in her apartment, pull a bentwood chair got from downstairs to the middle of the room, and sit, slouching just so—tranquil and patient—barely able to see over the windowsill. And she would watch Paco work, hustling in and out of her field of vision, dipping dishes into the piping-hot rinse and setting them aside to drain and dry. He would come out onto the stoop and sit with that Mason jar—she could hear the ice chips rattle and stir—or stand at the side edge of the stoop beside the dumpster, pissing—sometimes she'd catch him playing, spraying figure 8's and all. It is quite a game she plays, James, spying on him at work, speculating about the bulge in his pants and his cute little ass, watching him shake out when he's finished a piss. Then one night, she decides to turn the lights on and parade for him, she sipping from a beer mug of whiskey and water and ice that Paco supposes is tea—knowing full well she will catch Paco's attention.)

And then weeks later Paco catches sight of her pulling that chair up in front of the middle window in the darkened apartment; watches her sit as if fixed to the spot, staring at the back door of the Texas Lunch. He instantly, instinctively, freezes (sitting in the deepest dark with his back arched), his head turned, his eyes aloft, his kitchen apron drooping between his knees, with a cigarette and "strike anywhere" match in one hand and his juice jar in the other; he feels the excitement of his blood rushing through his body—and for a moment the pain in his back is gone—Paco thinking, How many days, weeks, has she been watching me?—him still beyond the light of the doorway, watching her spy. He has caught her at the game, slowly puts his cigarette in his mouth, poises the match in his hand, and lights it with his thumbnail.

Cathy, across the street and up the stairs, hears the rasping crackle of the match, sees the sparks glitter—sitting in that chair of hers a couple of steps back from the windows, with her legs pegged straight in front of her and her heels square on the thin, runway carpet between her writing desk and the long, itchy couch. And she's honest-to-God startled, James. He applies the flame to the cigarette and draws on it, and his whole face lights up, he's looking straight up at her, James, with eyes as clear as ice—she's caught, fair and square. And she blushes, thinking, Well goddamn, the gimp caught me—at the same time slouching more and sliding out of the chair. She crawls on her hands and knees into her bedroom, dresses in shorts and one of her father's hand-me-down dress shirts, and goes downstairs. He hears the clear click of her bedroom light switch, hears her rustling around getting dressed and leaving, pulling the door to, and regrets lousing up the nice little game they had going (grinning and shaking his head). He flips the cigarette away; it spins like crazy in a high arc, hits the stucco wall across the way, and explodes, showering sparkling ashes like fireworks. He chugalugs the rest of his orange drink, and goes back inside to finish his night's work.

Paco wanders over to the sink, begins another tubful of wash water and rinse, fetches a gray rubber bus pan from under the drainboard, and starts the last of his rounds. And just that minute a man walks into the front, dressed roughly, with well-weathered work boots and a jean jacket, a hitch-hiker's backpack (with a rolled-up bindle strapped to the top) over his shoulder. He takes a seat toward the back and settles his pack on the stool next to him. Ernest, mighty annoyed at some drifter waltzing in two minutes before closing, turns to the guy and says, "What'll you have?" And the guy slaps his hands together and rubs them so hard you hear the dry calluses. "What do you got that's hot?"

"Chili," Ernest says, sizing him up, reaching for a bowl and the oyster crackers before the guy can sniff.

"Well, okay, gimme a bowl of that chili con carne, a turkey club sandwich, and a large glass of tomato juice, *and* black coffee, *and* pie."

Paco comes out and passes behind Ernest, who is serving the drifter, and notices the pack and the bindle; when he comes back to refill his juice jar with a scoop of ice and more orange drink, he asks the guy, by way of conversation, where he's from, where he's bound.

The guy draws the bowl of chili to him (his name's Jesse), leans back, and says, "Been ever'where"; he puts a foot up on the frame of his backpack and begins to stir the thick, hot chili with a tablespoon to cool it down. "I've thumbed my ass from one end of this continent to the other. Seen the Alaska pipeline, for instance, and I'm here to tell you, my man"—he says to Paco, sliding his gaze to Ernest, who is vigorously scraping the griddle with his putty knife—"I'm here to tell you it ain't nothing but a damn pipe, for *all* you heard about it. I've pissed in the Grand Canyon—grand hole that! Spent the night in Beaver Falls, Goldsboro, French Lick—just to brag I been there. Et beans and franks at Phil's Drive-In in Corpus Christi, softshell crab as big as a Frisbee in Seattle, bouillabaisse thick as creamed soup," he says, spooning more oyster crackers into his chili and stirring it in, "at a rip-off dump called Jimmy's in Bos'on." Jesse begins putting chili and whole crackers in his mouth, washing everything down with gulps of coffee.

Ernest skims bits of onion and French fries and white fish fillet out of the hot oil, the scraps deep-fried to death. Paco ducks his head around the dangling-down, spiraled fly strip near the walk-in freezer—that fly strip lumpy with bugs—on his way to the back sink, and brushes against his black hickory cane and sets it swinging.

"Bought me a jeep one time," Jesse says, "and drove Pikes Peak. Swam off a raft on the Mississippi about half a day's drifting south of Muscatine, or some such place—no telling where we were at—me and this girl skinny-dipping. Been from Montpelier to Santa Fe, Yakima to Ocracoke Island,

Bemidji to Brownsville to Sault Sainte Marie," he says, pointing and leaning in one direction and another. He fingers his
turkey club sandwich, picking out the slices of pressed turkey.
(Ernest looks over his shoulder and catches Jesse picking at
his—Ernest's—sandwich and thinks to himself, Ernest, you
are always going to too much trouble for some people; perhaps
one day you'll learn.) "Where you from?" Jesse asks, taking
notice of Paco's rolling gait and cane swinging on its nail.

Paco halts at the back of the kitchen and sets down the
bus pan of dirty, sloppy dishes. Ever since the last snap of
cold in the earliest days of spring, months back, Paco has kept
to himself—working and walking home, dousing the pain
of his legs and back with endless double doses of muscle relaxers and anti-depressants. He has become something of a
public spectacle, hustling around the Texas Lunch in front of
the foundry workers and dairy farmers—everyone powerfully
curious about who he is and where it was he came from. Paco
washes his dishes, digging his arms past the elbows into that
lye-soap wash, smoking his Camels until the lip end is spit-
soaked and the corner of his mouth is greased with nicotine,
with his back to the dining room and not much minding what
goes on behind him ("What's back of you is behind, done,"
he'll tell you, James), except for Ernest and his sweet, homemade rosé wine and his stories about Guadalcanal and Iwo
Jima.

"Where *you* from?" Jesse repeats; louder, sitting up.

"What?" Paco says, unhooking his belt from the rim of
the washtub and coming out from behind the high counter at
back. Ernest stops his work, wiping the black griddle grease
from his scraper with a filthy sponge, standing ready to listen,
surprised that Paco is going to any trouble—thinking he's

finally going to hear something. "From?" Paco repeats. "Not around here. Wounded in the war," Paco says, expecting an argument. "Got fucked up at a place called Fire Base Harriette near Phuc Luc," and he stretches his arm and turns his head to the side to show off his scars. "Been in the hospital. Got out of the Army. Convalesced in one VA hospital after another. Cane's to help with the walking."

"Heard about Harriette," Jesse says, arch and astonished at the same time, but talking easy—breaking another handful of oyster crackers in his hands and sprinkling the crumbs onto his chili, brushing his hands clean so that we can hear again the dry swirl of the calluses. "Did *my*self a tour with the 173rd *Airborneski*! Iron fucking Triangle, Hobo Woods, the Bo Loi Woods. Lai Khe, An Loc, Cu Chi—back in the days when Ben Suc was still a ville. You heard of Ben Suc!" Paco had; Ernest had not. Jesse picks at the slices of turkey some more, dropping them into his mouth, eating bits of lettuce and tomato, too. "Airborneski, bub," he says, speaking to Ernest, "some crazy motherfuckers—to be sure, as the fella says. Training takes three weeks: first week they separate the men from the boys, second week they separate the men from the crazy motherfuckers, and the third week the motherfuckers jump. Swear to God," he says, beginning to wipe his mouth this way and that with his hands and fingers, "first time I flew in a plane was the first time I jumped. Made *twelve* jumps—good weather, bad; days, nights, noon times, you name it, bub—before I got aboard a plane that landed me anywhere. And *that* would have been Atlanta—there is some strange ginch in that town, don't ask me how come. And you know, when it's your turn to stand in the door and step out, you do *not* scream 'Geronimo!' Nobody but a shitbrained, candy-assed Hollywood fag would say something like that. When your turn comes to stand in the door and *go*, the jump-master lets you whoop any goddamned thing you've a mind to, any-fuckin'-thing that comes into your head—'Fuck the Army,' 'Kiss my ass,' 'Shit-shit-shit'—just sound off like you got a pair. He wants your young ass out the way," the guy says, while he's shaking lots of black pepper into his chili, grinning and looking at the ceiling. "It's kinda tasty, as the fella says, but all's you hear going down is the hiss. That and the static line clips clacking against the fuselage," he says, imagining the running lights blinking on the underside of the plane as he falls furiously to earth. "And pity your young ass if your chute don't open and you can't get your reserve to work. You'll be dropping past guys, flying like a rock flies, zoom! and your chute'll be streaming along behind you, going snappety-snap, poppety-pop, flappety-flap, like a fucking flag. And say you weigh 190 pounds like me. Well, you've got another 120, maybe 150 pounds strapped to you, so when you hit you'll be going so fast you just plain explode—*ka-plush*—and make a little hole in the ground all by yourself. Won't be enough left of you to butter a slice of bread, we used to say, and laughed while we said it. Sorry about that, bub," the guy says, and looks down, as if he's watched the whole affair, imagining the puff of dust, the splash, the tall grass spread back around the corpse.

"I did *my* motherfucker overseas back in '66–'67, in the old days, as the fella says, back when those jag-off housecats from CBS and NBC, and that kind, didn't get much past the far end of the lobby bar at the Honolulu Hilton. "Tell you, bub, fifty of them in a bowl wouldn't amount to a decent sit-down shit in an indoor shithouse rigged up with hot and cold potable water. You had to wonder what those guys were telling people, for *all* they were talking it up, because they would always wind up buddied up to the platoon shithead. Every time we'd see one of those newspaper clowns, we'd say something like 'Hey, spud, next time y'all come to the field, bring something with you in that fruit basket of yours' (they always had one of those big over-the-shoulder satchels or something like). 'Some decent, round-eyed pussy, for instance—if you can get a couple nice juicy pieces to jump into that sack of yours.' If those cornball chickenshits had hung around for more than a morning, they might have seen something. Would have seen some mean shit come down the pike, as the fella says." He looks out the doorway, toward the interstate. "Body count of a night as thick as high country timber; just as thick on the concertina wire as bugs on a bumper. Every swinging dick died proud, too, you could tell. I'll tell you one thing, those gooks gave as good as they got. We hated them and they hated us; some nights we fought each other for the pure hate of it. I humped my fucking share, but I guess you might know a little something about that," he says, meaning Paco. "But I swear, bub, when my tour was up I howdied around to everybody; told this one Alabama cracker of an NCO I ever saw him again, I didn't care where the fuck it was—Fenway Park, Furnace Creek, California, the goddamn lobby of the Palmer House Hotel—I'd beat him to a bloody nub with a fucking tire iron, even if I had to get him to stay put while I went out and got one. Sick, lame, or lazy; blind, crippled, or crazy—I can't remember which I was—didn't give a sweet fuck, I just wanted out of there. I came back to Fort Lewis right straight from Operation Cedar Chips (or some such fucking nonsense as that), got my discharge and my pay, and I say to myself, I got to see what this fucking country's made of. And I've been seeing the sights ever since, been looking for a place to cool out."

Paco comes by to fetch the chili pot and offers the guy what's left, filling his bowl to the brim. Ernest and Paco work, making headway cleaning up for the night while the drifter eats, talking between bites—looking back at Paco scrubbing pots, and forward toward Ernest checking the till.

"Lived for the better part of a year in an antique cabin in the Bitterroot Range on the Montana–Idaho border. Had a 30-acre meadow that flowered over the whole summer, a creek not a hundred meters from the porch, this big-ass wild orchard, and a split-rail fence with a gate that hadn't been moved since before I was born, I'm sure. There was a elk herd would come and graze, and you goddamned near had to shoo them away to get to the outhouse. Lived there the better part of a year; scrounged work; stayed just as stoned as stoned could be; drank like a fish, whiskey and bourbon and all that good Scotch—I figured if I stayed stoned and falling-down drunk, I wouldn't be held responsible if I fucked anybody up. Let my beard and hair go all to hell—by the time I was ready to come down out of the Bitterroot for good (a body do get squirrelly, some), I was downright fucking ugly. But I had the time to 'set and drank and thank,' as the fella says, and I came to know something, and it is this," and he threw back his head so that his brown ponytail swayed behind him, laughed and growled with a sudden, deep, and sharply bitter voice, "primo is that I'm goddamned sorry I never got a chance to beat the shit out of an MP or tell General Schistkoff or Sheetrock, or whatever his name was, to fuck off. And secundo, I am a fully stamped, qualified *slab* animal—successful species—who made it out of their fucking lab." And he jerked his head down again and banged his tablespoon on the linoleum counter—those solid cracks of metal clear and dull-sounding.

"Been waiting for one of those mouthy, snappy-looking little girlies from some rinky-dink college to waltz up and say"—and his voice rises into a fey falsetto, squeaking as though he's rehearsed it—" 'You one of them *vet'rans*, ain'cha? Killed all them mothers and babies. Raped all them women, di'n'cha'—*I only got two hands, lady!*—'Don't touch me, *so* nasty,' as the fella says, 'I ain't putting out for you, *buster*, not so much as a handshake!' Okay by me, girlie," Jesse says, looking straight up, " 'cause I got seventeen different kinds of social diseases—runny sores and all swoll up and everything dripping smelly green pus all the time, no telling what and all. And when this happens—this conversation with this here girlie—I'm gonna grab her up by the collar of her sailor suit (or whatever the fuck they're parading around in these days), slap her around a couple times, flip her a goddamned dime— got the fuckin' money right here," he says, and leans back so he can pat his pants pockets, "and say, 'Here, Sweet Chips, give me a ring in a couple of years when you grow up.' " He looks around and squirms, his face warm with suppressed anger and his stomach warm with peppered chili. He licks the tablespoon and rattles it around in his tepid coffee, pouring in heaping teaspoons of sugar, tapping his well-weathered work boots against the stool pedestal—his lanky, rangy body suddenly eager to move.

"I just can't wait till they build a fuckin' Vietnam Monument." (This, James, years before anybody ever thought of one.) "That's one edifice I'd pay money, gladly, to see. But that bunch of good old boys, big-shot lawyers, ex-Marine Corps heroes, ring-knocking fighter jocks who can't get enough of that boomin' and zoomin', as the fella says, and General goddamn William Westmoreland his own self (guys that never hit a straight lick or humped as much as a single click their whole lives)—they'll fuck around and fart around and grab-ass around, and jack that thing up so's it'll be some horse's ass of a hero's statue. They'll pass the hat under Chrysler's nose, *and* General Dynamics's *and* Hughes Aircraft's *and* Boeing's, just raking it in. Then they'll get some half-hacked Boy Scout lieutenant ('All my life I've wanted to lead *brave* men to *victory* in a *desperate* battle!'), who's got a dick about the size of your thumb and a peach-fuzz mustache, a wrinkled-up bush hat and some godawful PX *cee*-gar, but, when it comes right down to the button, don't know his ass from a hole in the ground. He'll pose, fucking-new-guy-fashion, with this cheerleader, frat-boy grin on his face, as much as to say, 'Hi, Mom! I'm fucking-A *proud* to be dead! Semper *Fi*, Mac!' He'll be standing on an effigy of a Purple Heart, with his knees all loosy-goosy, like he's surfing, but holding a corpse of a dead GI heavenward, as if just that minute he clean-and-jerked it. And you got to know that statue will be some dipped-in-shit, John Wayne crapola that any grunt worth his grit and spit is going to take one good look at and say, 'Boo-*she-it*! Ah mean *bull*shit!' They'll mount that John Wayne-looking thing on a high pedestal and set it out by the road so the lifers and gun nuts can cruise by in their Jeep campers and Caddies and see it good and plain. Or they can park and stand real close (dressed in their K-Mart cammies), and get a lump in their throats and all creamy between the thighs, feeling sad and sorrowful, remembering and admiring the old days.

"Well, my own design for a memorial is somewhat more theatrical, *and* fragrant, as the fella says," says Jesse, reaching over the counter for the coffeepot and pouring himself another cup. "Get yourself a couple acres of prime Washington, D.C., property, see, somewhere in line with the Reflecting Pool." He turns and squints at an imaginary plumb line down the row of stools and out the door. "That way the Congress can stand on the Capitol steps, sight down the Mall, the Washington Monument, the whole fucking length of the Reflecting Pool, out through the columns of the Lincoln Memorial, across the Potomac River, and up the slopes of the Arlington National Cemetery, and admire their work; thousands upon thousands of rows of fucked-up lives. And *there* will be the Vietnam War Monument. Chop a couple acres off the top of some grassy knoll. Cover it with Carrara marble, bub, the whitest stone God makes. Engrave the marble with the names of all the Vietnam War Dead—every swinging dick, as the fella says. Arrange the names any goddamned way you've a mind to," he says, holding his hand up and looking out the door as if he's standing on the Capitol steps, superintending. "First come, first served might not be a bad idea. Then in the middle of all that marble put a big granite bowl, a big mortar-looking thing about the size of a three-yard dump truck. Collect thousands of hundred-dollar bills, funded by an amply endowed trust fund, say, to keep the money a-coming. Then gather every sort of 'egregious' excretion that can be transported across state lines from far and wide—

chickenshit, bullshit, bloody fecal goop, radioactive dioxin sludge, kepone paste, tubercular spit, abortions murdered at every stage of fetal development—I don't know what and all. Shovel all that shit into that granite bowl and mix in the money by the tens of thousands of dollars. Stir it all together —build a goddamn scaffolding and use galley oars if that suits you. Then back way up and hose down the sod. Get it good and soggy; nice and mucky. Then advertise. 'Come one! Come all! Any and all comers may fish around in that bowl of shit and keep any and all hundred-dollar bills they come across,' barehanded, but first they must take off their shoes, roll up their trousers, slug through that knee-deep muck, and wind up slopping it all over that marble.

"I tell you, bub, we could celebrate the grand opening with an ABC Wide World of Sports Battle of the Network Stars Celebrity Spectacular—giggly, tittied-up sit-com pussies, he-man soap-opera fags, and a couple late-night talk-show shills. The whole thing done under strings of carnival lights in elim-ination heats, while Howard Cosell, Evel Knievel, and Martha Raye do the play-by-play and the color commentary."

Paco and Ernest have to laugh at *that*, James, grinning at the grinding and raucous bitter irony of it. Jesse reaches into one of the side pockets of his backpack—having to rest his chin on the counter and feel with his fingers, rummaging around and rolling his eyes—and comes up with a quart jar of brewer's yeast and a small bottle of vitamin pills and cap-sules.

Paco, too, moves, coming forward to collect another tub-ful of dishes and pouring himself a refill of orange drink. "How you get around?" Paco asks while he holds the bus tray against his stomach with one hand and collects Jesse's dishes, the steam-table utensils, and pots and pans, piling everything high. "Hitchhiking, I mean. How you get around?" he says, and makes a big circle above his head with the large round artist's brush that Ernest butters the toast with.

Jesse spoons brewer's yeast into his tomato juice with the same spoon he used for the chili and for stirring his coffee.

"You in a hurry?" he says, screwing the top back on the old mayonnaise jar of yeast—"Stick to the interstates. Local roads are for yokels and rookies and yoboes. GIs ought to wear their uniforms. I swear on my mother's grave I saw a U.S. Marine thumbing his way out of Norfolk in his dress-fuckin'-blues—gloves and this unbelievable spit shine and I don't know what and all—and the dude got a ride from some civilian in a funeral procession. You got to *look* clean, even if you stink to high heaven, and smile, bub. Hold your thumb straight above your head—you're on the ramp above and away from the traffic, remember—as far as your arm will reach, so the suckers down there will see you, dig? And it helps if you jump up and down. Now, you want to make a little sign? Sure, go ahead and make yourself a little sign, but keep it simple and make the letters *big*—NYC, WASH DC, UCLA, FLA, FT L'WOOD. Never-oh-never write CALIF OR BUST, or NORTH, and so on. Believe you me, nobody fuckin' cares. It's a real kiss of death, as the fella says. And never travel with a girl. There's something people don't like about the look of it; too many rip-offs, maybe. And when you get pissed off, never-oh-never make an obscene gesture. May the Lord have pity on your sorry-assed pecker. That geek may stop, slam his Buick in reverse, and back all the way up that ramp where you're standing under that big sign that reads:

NO FOOT TRAFFIC
ON ROADWAY

He'll whip out some monster .44 he keeps under his seat, daydreaming about dumbshit wiseacres like you, and blow you away with one round, as the fella says. And all's they're gonna find of you is the toenails.

"Now, if you're having a hard time, whistle. There's something buddy-buddy about the look on your face when you whistle—don't ask me why. Just don't look slaphappy," he says, loud, making sure Paco, busy with the last round of dishes, can hear. "Slaphappy people look stupid, loony—and drivers think you're on something, I guess. Above all, *look* interested and intelligent—bright-eyed and bushy-tailed—even if your ass is dragging. And Lord, *Lord*, when a ride stops for you, grab your shit and get hustling. Only a total screaming asshole waits for a slowpoke. But for God's sake, don't hop right in. Check a ride out first; you might wind up with your bootie busted, otherwise. Look the guy up and down—women ain't gonna stop for you, so don't worry about that. If it looks cool, help yourself. And for Christ's sake, be grateful—it sure beats the shit out of walking. I've humped mine, and then some, believe you me. But you being a grunt, I guess you know about that."

"Some," says Paco, and laughs.

"Thank the man," Jesse says. "But don't get palsy-walsy. Carry a rucksack—you look too bummy otherwise, like some slack-assed, shit-for-brains hippie. I carry a small hunting knife in a scabbard, and keep it strapped to the side of my ruck. Not to be threatening or anything, just so everybody knows I ain't gonna tolerate no funny business. Showing that to folks in a casual way saves a lot of peculiar conversation, as the fella says. Always travel with a ruck, because when you hit a gas station you get a chance to take a whore's bath and change some of your clothes. And, bub," he says to Paco, loud, "you've been to the field enough to know you will think you died and went to heaven when you stumble on a washroom with a hot-water tap. A supreme pleasure, as the fella says, but real rare."

Ernest comes down the way, hustling Paco back to work. "That may well be so," he says, "but let's finish this work and go home." They settle up for the chili, the sandwich, and the rest—Jesse counting out the money from a rawhide coin purse; Ernest toting up the day's receipts from the till and tucking them into his money belt. "You finish, lock up, and I'll see you in the morning—like always," he says to Paco, and leaves, turning out all but the last of the lights.

Jesse offers to help Paco finish, taking a kitchen rag to the countertops, the stools, the tables and chairs.

And they work for a time, Paco rattling around with the last of the cook pots, that one light bulb over the sink harsh; Jesse efficiently dry-wiping the plastic covers of the chairs, dawdling to inspect Ernest's collection of kitchen clocks—the light in the dining room much diminished. Then suddenly he tosses the rag down and turns toward the high counter at the back, behind which Paco works, and says, "It was a shitty thing that happened at Harriette"—as if he's been turning that event over in his mind—the news of it and the impact—and has been trying to think of something to say about *it*, and Paco, since he walked into the place. And here it comes.

Paco swirls rinse water around in the 10-quart stewpot, straightens up, and says, "Doctors told me I was the only one of ninety-three guys"—remembering how the crusted muck pulled at his hair, the suffocating dread of lingering death for almost two days, the flat-out astonishment of the Bravo Company medic.

"Well, ain't you bitter about that?" Jesse says.

Paco pours out the sudsy rinse and sets the pot down to drain-dry. He comes out into the dark kitchen and dining room, standing in a throbbing agony, silhouetted by the nightlight of the walk-in freezer. It takes him a moment to find Jesse in the dark, standing among the dining tables. "I've sat up many a night brooding about that, rolling that around in my mouth, so to say, and yeah, I expect I'm as bitter as bitter can be, more than tongue can tell most likely. But I'll tell you something else: I'm just glad to be here—isn't that what Thurman Munson says?

"Say now, you think you'll stick around any?" Paco asks, meaning, Let's have a drink and sit and shoot the shit.

"Naw," Jesse says, meaning, No offense, but I've got to get a move on. "There's plenty of good traveling at night now I've got something to eat. Good chili." Jesse wrings out the rag and lays it over the edge of the high counter. Then he snatches up his rucksack, swings it over his shoulder, and stands by the back door.

"Where you bound?" Paco asks, standing there cramped with side stitches.

"West—Cheyenne," Jesse says, hefting his gear, leaving. "Then south—Taos, 'where Texas skis,' as the fella says." He stands on the greasy concrete stoop with the screen door open, looking inside at Paco hanging up his apron, taking down his cane. "You take extra *good* care of yourself," he says, not knowing what else to say.

"I will do that!" Paco says, looking back at Jesse—his eyes and beard sparkling in the light of the street; the highlights of his face glowing in the warm air. "And don't *you* step in any shit. Hear?" Paco says as Jesse goes down the steps and turns the corner at the sidewalk. Paco locks the back door, rattling the lock to make sure it's secure, and crosses the street, home—glancing up at Cathy's windows and those billowing sheers. He watches Jesse walking out of town—his well-weathered work boots grinding in the roadside gravel; walking out into the countryside along that well-done, two-lane state road, contrary to his own advice—his gait smooth; whistling a Strauss waltz ("The Emperor Waltz," as it happens, James):

working the tune on the blow and draw, both.

6. Good Morning to You, Lieutenant. We can

stand at the crest of the town's one good hill, James, and
pause and get quiet and comfortable and still, and listen to the
night sounds. At this late hour of the night the tranquil murmuring hum of the river, cascading over the rock-and-concrete
spillway under the bridge, yonder, is almost the only sound to
be heard. That constant rush of water is the hush that has
lulled many a strapping newborn infant to sleep in its time;
the last sobering sound heard suddenly, abruptly, in many a
deathbed room, as clean and even and smooth as the curl in the
neck of a glass cider jug.

But that is not the only sound to be heard late at night,
James. We can sit on the thick slate curb, under the parkway
walnuts, and hear the squeak of wicker chairs; the tumble of
ice melting to slivers in glasses of Coke and tea and whiskey;
the whisper of bedroom conversation that is all hisses, and the
snapping and popping of buttons; women flapping and flutter-
ing their summer dress fronts; the shrill squeal of children

racing through swirling clouds of fireflies, a game better than tag; someone spitting on dry pavement; the snick-snick-snick of a loose pack of town dogs trotting across the schoolyard blacktop. Then comes the sound that all but stops the others, even the dogs—the step, tap-step, of that gimpy kid wounded in the war, that guy Paco, walking home from the Texas Lunch.

All those night sounds bristle, brushing back and forth under the trees, and everyone who's sitting back, listening, hears. And we hear, don't we, James—the river pouring over the spillway, the ring of jar lids, the giggles, the clear click of the cast-brass tip of Paco's cane.

And the girl with the rooms across the hall from the top of the stairs at the Geronimo Hotel listens, too. The girl, James —her name Cathy, remember—small-breasted and bony-armed, built like a smooth-faced, tallish boy. Nowadays, when-ever Paco sees her, she's wearing one of her father's dress shirts with the cuffs rolled a time or two to the middle of her forearms, the shirttails loose around her thighs, with a starched collar as stiff as a military uniform tunic. Nearly every night now (these the deadest, hottest nights in the deadest, hottest weeks of August and September, James), the girl will sit on the broad, dusty sill of the alley window, with her small, clean feet drawn up under her, and lean her cheek against the filthy screen (her spying game done with; "No fun," she'll tell you facetiously, James, in a parody of pouting). She listens the way a meditative person will gaze into a bon-fire. She perks her ears with deliberate intent, listening ever so keenly for the sharp click of Paco's black hickory cane on the asphalt, and the sure and steady, slightly off-rhythm of his walk—step, tap-step. Her moist, sparkling eyes will dart this way and that round the room, and she'll glance out the window, rubbing the cool, smooth, nut-brown skin of her knee (her whole body as brown as buttered toast, James), with the breezy heat of the tin-and-tar roof rising in her face, and she'll count the courses of smoothed railroad brick in the alley below. She will stare absentmindedly at her own fingers as she strums a limp gold anklet with manicured fingernails. She will imagine Paco's hands, bleached white and water wrinkled, his sour, sweat-soaked T-shirt clinging to the hard flat of his belly, that glazed-over, glossy look in his eyes— which in most folks is simple work weariness, you understand.

Every night now, when she hears the click of his cane on the asphalt change to the mellow, hollow thump of the hotel stoop, she will uncurl herself and crawl crablike across her bed. She will primp on the move and brush herself down, using her fingers for a whisk, smoothing that lime- or peach-or cocoa-colored dress shirt (opened a couple of buttons at the neck), and strike a pose leaning against the warm wood of her door. Sometimes she will hold the door open just so far, with her head and shoulders poked into the hall as though she's just out of the shower and still wet and doesn't want to drip on the hallway rug, but the front of her shirt will be nearly all unbuttoned, and there will be enough light shining down her front to be teasing, enticing. And sometimes she will put just her head in the light, with her body to one side behind the door, and she'll have a glittering gleam in her eye, as though she doesn't have a stitch on. And you've got to know, James, that some nights she doesn't, but those nights are for *her* benefit, not Paco's, because being buck naked when she smiles that smirk down at him makes her feel so goosy and juicy, and some nights she can't help but giggle. She will wait for Paco to come in the front and stop at the bottom of the stairway, standing stoop-shouldered, leaning so heavily on that goddamned cane some nights it will bow. She will wait for him to raise his eyes, looking up through the railing rungs, and see her in the dim amber light of the several head-high hallway sconces—the light shining on the smooth, browned skin of her legs and face, looking like dry, oval slivers of yellowed antique ivory, the air musty and rich like a bowl of sun-warmed, softening fruit, and the skylight over the deep, high stairwell nearly painted over with roofing tar.

She will stir slightly, waiting to see that look in his eye that is unmistakable in a man who has not been to bed with a woman for a long time. And Paco will nod, almost imperceptibly, and *then* will begin the race, the *new* game, the struggle to get to the top of the stairs before she slips back into her room and closes the door. It is the one solid rule of their game, James. If Paco can get so much as the tip of his cane in the door before she shuts it, he can come in ("You can fuck me, sugar!").

Paco has struggled up those stairs many a warm night, ass-whipped tired, his legs tingling and throbbing, wobbly even, his feet soaked and sore—that goddamned lye-soap rash on his arms as red as rope burns. Washing dishes by hand ain't no pleasure and it ain't no joke, James.

And tonight, just like any other night, getting in Cathy's doorway doesn't happen. She's not there, but he's not interested either. Oh no. Tonight he comes up the street and into the hotel, hits the stairs, and just keeps coming. Tonight Paco has been sitting on the damp, hard clay of the riverbank near the spillway, listening to the skinny-dippers horsing around in the sand-bottomed shallows downriver from the old railroad trestle, drinking quart after quart of decently warm beer fetched from Rita's half the night—waiting for the air to cool —and there's no telling what time it is.

He tops the stairs and limps along the hallway to the left with his skeleton key in one hand and his cane in the other (the roof rafters crackling overhead, cooling; the chain of the HOTEL sign twisting and squeaking—on rainy nights we can hear the neon sizzle and buzz). He works his door open, steps in, and closes it behind him with a slow and heavy click (as firm and final a sound as we are liable to hear in that hotel, James). The hall light vanishes from the room except for that flat, slender sliver under the door, which is no bigger than a piece of oak lath. Paco squeezes his head against the warm wood of the door (the smelly varnish almost gooey to the touch), squeezing his eyes shut with the pure relief of being home, taking a bit of a breather. He's got a still, stuffy, smothering little room, with a crumbling 8 x 10 linoleum sheet, a ragged mahogany dresser with the veneer shredding to splinters, and a coffee-colored bedstead with a brown bedspread— all that woodwork smelling of solid old age. There is a scum of dust in all the corners, and fuzzy wallpaper you would swear was flocked if you brushed against it in the dark. He rattles around in his darkened room, peeling off his T-shirt, unbuckling his belt and unzipping his fly, scooting his pants down, skivvies and all. Then he flops on his creaking bed, the way drunks do. His head and arms loll this way and that, and his legs hang over the edge of the bed with the balls of his feet brushing the floor. He sets his hands wide on the raspy, graying sheets, stares *hard* at the curling chips of paint above his head, then takes a good long breath, and, with a sudden, sharp exhalation, lifts his legs onto the bed. And it's godawful painful, James. Sometimes the pain shoots straight up his legs and thighs into his back and arms (he can hear the pins and screws grinding against the bone some nights; oh, the grimacing squint wrinkles he will have). The very tips of his fingers tingle as though someone has pricked them.

He takes a long moment to settle in—to get his sore, throbbing legs and the small of his back just so among the lumps. The air is hot and heavy all around him, and the sheets are as itchy and scratchy as snapping-dry flannel. (Everything has been warm and sticky and uncomfortable all day, every day and all the night through for weeks now, James. Bread won't rise right. Beer foam looks pale and greasy and slippery. Your clothes bunch thickly at the crotch and cling to your back and down under your arms, for instance, and folks are awkward and bitchy and ill-tempered most of the time.)

We can take a pause now, and lean over Paco's thighs and knees and calves, James, even in the little light of his room; there *is* a slice of moon, a 40-watt back-porch light, and the glow of a yellow hall light reflected into the room under the door—this faint and burdensomely warm and oppressive light that gives his room a welcome and intimate air nonetheless, as still and smothering a place as we are likely to come across these warm and stuffy nights, unrelieved by comfort. If we lean down, we can see the many razor-thin surgical scars, the bone-fragment scars (going every which way) the size of pine-stump splinters, the puckered burn scars (from cooked-off ammunition) looking as though he's been sprayed with a shovelful of glowing cinders, the deadened, discolored ring of skin at the meatiest part of his thigh, where the Bravo Company medic wound the twisted tourniquet, using Paco's own bandanna, though the time for a tourniquet had long passed. The sallow, thin-faced medic slapped the crook of Paco's elbow to get a vein, and Paco and half the company could hear his grumble: "Come *on*, you dumbshit grunt motherfucker, give me a *goddamn* vein," and Paco's arm stung like a son-of-a-bitch—the medic's dog tags jangling in Paco's face. And if we look closely at Paco's arm, we can see the scar of the gouge at the inside of his forearm, the size of a pencil stub, where the catheter ripped loose when those shit-for-brains Bravo Company litter bearers dropped Paco down a rain-slick footpath, litter and all. ("You goddamned bullshit fucking Bravo Company Jesus Christ, I hope you motherfuckers all die shit!" Paco whispered, and cried.)

We could lean down and take a good hard look, and see all that, James, even in this little light. We could back away, now that we know what we're looking at, and those scars will seem to wiggle and curl, snapping languidly this way and that, the same as grubs and night crawlers when you prick them with the barb of a bait hook. But it is only an illusion, James, a sly trick of the eye—the way many a frightful thing in this world comes alive in the dimmest, whitest moonlight, the cleanest lamplight.

Paco lies on his bed, trying to nod off, trying to get as comfortable as the muggy air and sweaty-filthy sheets and teasing, tickling ache will allow, but out the window—kitty-corner to his—Paco hears Cathy honey-fucking the everlasting daylights out of some guy (*Marty-boy*, she calls him). There's no mistaking that sloppy, glucking sound, the bed squeaking effortlessly and meekly, the lovely sounds of their fucking filling the room (the way a cat's purring will fill a room, James). Marty-boy eases in and out of her, his buttocks working, his ankles crossed and the dry bottoms of his feet reaching over the foot of her bed. He bends his head down and licks her pearly breasts; Cathy arching up, holding him to her with her hands and heels, really enjoying all that.

Fucking the girl is something Paco has dreamed about over and over, sprawled spread-eagle on his creaking bed, with his flaccid cock (slashed with scars) flopped to one side of his thighs—oh, how his back would ache on those nights—his pubic hair fluffy and prickly, almost crackling in the heat, like dry grass.

Paco is furiously jealous—Marty-boy's clean haircut and the undulating smoothness of his back (not a mark on the son-of-a-bitch, James); Cathy's vigorous huffing and puffing, with her face squinched up, and her thrashing that fluffy hair from side to side, whipping it across Marty-boy's face; and him squinting severely, his whole body shuddering with the effort. Paco doesn't have to strain any to hear—can practically slide his hand and arm out his windowsill, over the nicotine burns and coffee-cup rings, lean out a little and fingertip-touch the top of her hair. Cathy sighs slowly and calmly and soothingly—content, Paco thinks to himself (his cock getting solid, jerking stiffly in the air)—brimful of peace and pleasure.

Now Cathy heard Paco fiddle with his key in the lock; heard him fumbling around in his dingy little room; smelled the very beer on his breath. And so now with each slippery thrust she stretches her thin little neck and exhales audibly toward the window. She pulls on Marty-boy's pale, shuddering hips—clawlike, with sedately manicured nails—and sways from side to side with her heels spiked into the mattress.

Then she's swinging her legs in the air—the hairs glittering—now staccato, now languidly, in a fresh surfeit of pleasure; now pummeling the small of his back in a frenzy with the callused points of her heels (with her thin, pinkish tongue between her teeth and a slaphappy grin on her face, as though to say, I get a nice little kick from teasing that gimp, but the fucking is nice and I love it, too).

Paco wishes Marty-boy (some primary-education major from the Wyandotte Teachers College, the same as Cathy) to hell and gone. Paco sweats up a storm trying to wish himself sober, trying to wish himself up from his bed and out of his room (side-stepping down the hallway in purposeful slow motion—toe-heel-toe—his hands skimming flat against the wall for guidance, balance). Paco has the incredible, shivering urge to sneak into Cathy's room and stalk up behind Marty-boy as bold as brass, grab him by the hips and yank him off, shake him out and set him aside, as if he were a mannequin. (Marty-boy would stand there astonished, wiggling like a big old bass snagged at the side of the head with a treble hook and dragged ashore—flabbergasted.) Cathy would be pulling at her own hair by then; grinding her hips in the air, straining her legs and belly, her pussy luminescent with lubrication. Paco imagines that he climbs onto the bed between her legs, stretching out above her. He imagines, too, that he slides into her as easily as a warm, clean hand slips into a greased glove; that she whimpers grotesquely, encircling him at once with her arms and legs, holding him to her like warm covers.

By this time Paco's cock is iron hard and feels as big as a Coke bottle. And he's just a man like the rest of us, James, who wants to fuck away all that pain and redeem his body. By fucking he wants to ameliorate the stinging ache of those dozens and dozens of swirled-up and curled-round, purple scars, looking like so many sleeping snakes and piles of ruined coins. He wants to discover a livable peace—as if he's come up a path in a vast evergreen woods, come upon a comfortable cabin as solid as a castle keep, and approached, calling, "*Hello the house*," been welcomed in, given a hot and filling dinner, then shown a bed in the attic (a pallet of sweet dry grass and slim cedar shavings) and fallen asleep.

Paco lies on his back, smelling the starched linen on her bed, Cathy's eau de cologne and pink talc, the pungent tin-and-tar porch roof—the powerfully rank sweetness of their sweat. Paco stares up at the darkened ceiling and the curled chips of paint that hang down as thick as a shedding winter shag. Then abruptly, he remembers Gallagher's Bangkok R & R tattoo, the red-and-black dragon that covered his forearm from his wrist to his elbow (that tattoo a goddamned work of art, everyone said, a regular fucking masterpiece). He sees the tattoo, then suddenly remembers the rape of the VC girl, and the dreams he has had of the rape.

He winces and squirms; his whole body jerks, but he cannot choose but remember.

Gallagher had this girl by the hair. She wasn't just anybody, you understand, James—not some dirt farmer's wife or one of those godawful ugly camp-following whores; not some poor son-of-a-bitch's tagalong sister pestering everyone with her whining; not some rear-rank slick-sleeve private (who doesn't know dismounted, close-order drill from shit and Shinola), who pushed a pencil or wrapped bandages, and smiled big and pretty when the Swedish journalists shot through on the grand tour. No, James, she was as hard a hardcore VC as they come (by the look of the miles on her face). She had ambushed the 1st platoon's night listening post just shy of first light and shot two of them dead (the third guy had tackled her when she ran, and beat the shit out of her bringing her in), and now the company was hunkered down, wet and sullen, plenty pissed off, waiting for the dust-off and a couple of body bags. Gallagher was nibbling on a bar of Hershey's Tropical Chocolate (the color of dogshit) and sipping heavily chlorinated canteen water, watching her squatting on her haunches, wolfing down a C-ration can of ham and eggs some fucking new guy had given her—wolfing it down with a plastic spoon and her thumb—and finally Gallagher had had enough. The next thing you know, James, he had her by the hair and was swearing up a storm, hauling her this way and that (the spit bubbles at the corners of his mouth slurring his words) through the company to this brick-and-stucco hooch off to one side of the clearing that's roofless and fucked over with mortar and artillery hits up one side and down the other.

Paco sees wiseacre ("Fuck-you-up-boy") Gallagher haul that girl through the night laager; sees this dude and that peel off from their night positions and follow across the hard, bare clay, smacking their lips to a fare-thee-well—there's a bunch of guys in that company want a piece of *that* gook. Gallagher waltzes her into the room at the side, no doubt a bedroom. And the whole time the girl looked at that red-and-black tattoo out of the corners of her eyes like a fretted, hysterical dog. She could see only the slick-sweated tail, curled and twisted and twined around itself, and the stumpy, lizardlike legs; the long, reddish tongue curled around the snout and head and the long, curving neck and forelegs, but she could not see that much because of the way Gallagher had her by the hair.

(Take your hand, James, and reach around the top of your head, grab as much hair as you can grab in one hand and *yank*, then press that arm tight against the side of your head and look over, hard, at your arm out of the corners of your eyes. That's as much of Gallagher's arm as the girl saw.)

The hooch was claustrophobic, with thick walls and small rooms, and smelled like an old wet dog. Gallagher and the rest of us reeked sourly of issue mosquito repellent and camouflage stick and marijuana, sopping-wet clothes and bloody jungle rot (around the crotch and under our arms). The girl smelled of jungle junk and cordite—gunpowder, James—and piss.

(If the zip had been a man, we would not have bothered with the motherfucker, you understand that, don't you? Gallagher, or whoever, would have grabbed that son-of-a-bitch by his whole head of hair—that zip staring at the twined and twisted and curlicued red-and-black tail of that Bangkok R & R tattoo, knowing jolly well it was going to be the last thing he'd be likely to get a good clean look at in *this* life. Gallagher would have dragged him over to that hooch, jerking him clean off his feet every other step, snatching his head this way and that for good measure, grumbling through his teeth about the one and only way to put the chill on gooks. We would have taken him around to the side, held him straight-backed against the beat-to-hell brick-and-stucco hooch wall—the zip's eyes that big and his poor little asshole squeezed tighter than a four-inch wad of double sawbucks. That cocksucker would have been pounded on till his face was beat to shit; till our arms were tired—"Anybody else want a poke at him? Going once. Twice. Three fuckin' times." Then someone would have held him while Jonesy pulled out his pearl-handled straight razor just as slow and catlike and quiet as a barber commencing to trim around your ears. Jonesy would have flicked that sucker open with a flashy snap, showing that puffy-eyed, bloody-faced zip four inches of the goddamnedest Swedish steel he's likely to come across, and then just as slow and calm and cool as you'd have a melon, James, Jonesy would have slit that zip's throat from nine to three. And he wouldn't have cut him the way he snipped ears; wouldn't have cut him the way he whittled booby-trap tripwire stakes for Paco; no, he'd cut him with a slow sweep of the hand and arm, the same as reapers sweep those long-handled scythes—that long, bare-armed motion that makes their sweat pop and the yellow wheat lie back in thick shocks. Beautiful and terrible.

The razor cut would have bled horrible abundance, the zip's life gushing from his neck in terrific spurts, with him watching it, hardly believing—his face wax-white. It would have been as though he'd been garroted, good and proper hard; only, the razor cut would have hissed and bubbled and gurgled the way strangling with a wire simply cannot.

You've got to understand, James, that if the zip had been a man we would have punched on him, then killed him right then and there and left him for dead.)

So Gallagher hauled the woman off by the hair, and she looked as hard as hard can be at that red-and-black tattoo. And she was naked from the waist up, but nothing much to look at, so no one was much looking at her, and she was flailing her arms, trying to gouge Gallagher's eyes out, and swinging her legs, trying to kick him in the balls, but Gal-

lagher was doing a pretty good job of blocking her punches
and holding her back (was a wrestler, Gallagher was). She
screamed in Viet that no one understood but could figure out
pretty well, "*Pig.* You *pig.* GI beaucoup number ten goddamned shit-eating fucking pig. I *spit* on you!" Gallagher
dodged and bobbed and weaved, and chuckled, saying, "Sure,
Sweet Pea, sure!" He pulled her—arms flailing, legs kicking,
screaming that hysterical gibberish at the top of her lungs.
And everybody in the whole ballpark knew they weren't going
in that hooch to argue who can throw the blandest brush-back
pitch—Lyle Walsh or Dub Patterson. Even Lieutenant John
Ridley Stennett (Dartmouth, 1967) knew, for a refreshing
fucking change. Good morning to you, Lieutenant!

We took her into the side room, and there wasn't much
of the roof left, but there were chunks of tiles and scraps of
air-burst howitzer shrapnel, and the ass end of some bullshit
furniture littered around. You walked on the stone parquet
floor and the crumbs of terra-cotta roofing tile, and it crunched
—like glass would grind and snap and squeak underfoot. That
hooch was a ruin, James, a regular stone riot of ruin. Gallagher
and the girl, Jonesy and Paco and the rest of us, stood in the
brightening overcast (more like intense, hazy glare) that
made us squint involuntarily, as though we were reading a
fine-print contract.

Jonesy took a long stretch of black commo wire and
whipped a handful of it into the open air. It looped high over
the ridgepole and came down, smacking Paco in the leg. Gallagher and Paco held the girl down firmly while Jonesy tied
her wrists together behind her back, then hauled on that wire
the same as if he were hoisting the morning colors, just as
crisp and snappy as the book says—*The Manual of Arms,*

James, the twenty-two-dash-five, we called it. The girl had to bend over some or dislocate both arms, so she bent down over this raw wood thing about the size of a kitchen table. The girl was scared shitless, chilly and shuddering, glossy and greasy with sweat, and was all but tempted to ask them as one human being to another not to rape her, not to kill her, but she didn't speak English.

There was considerable jostling and arm punching, jawing and grab-ass back and forth, and everyone formed a rough line, so just for that moment Paco got to stand there and take a long look. A peasant girl, not more than fourteen, say, or sixteen. And by the look of her back she had worked, *hard*, every day of her life. She was not beefy, though. None of the Viets were big, but then sharecropping doesn't tend to turn out strapping-big hale-and-hearty offspring. Ask someone who knows shit from shit and Shinola about farming, James, and he will tell you that sharecropping is a long, hard way to get down to business and get some. The dumbest dumbshit on the face of this earth (who knows just enough about farming to follow a horse around with a coal shovel) knows that sharecropping sucks; knows you can't spend your life sharing your crop with *yourself*, much less split it between you and the Man. But who knows, maybe Viets enjoyed being gaunt and rickety, rheumy and toothless. Maybe. They got along well enough on forty-and-found—what they grew and what they scrounged—and it was a long row to hoe, James. Viet sharecroppers ate rice and greens and fish heads, and such as that—whatever they caught, whatever they could lay their bare hands on.

Jonesy stepped up behind the girl, took out his pearl-handled straight razor with a magician's flourish—acting real gaudy and showy the way he could—and slit her flimsy black pants from the cuffs to the waistband, just the same as you'd zip a parka right to your chin. Then he hauled off and hoisted her up another notch or two for good measure, until her shoulders turned white (clear on the other side of the laager Lieutenant Stennett heard the commo wire squeak against the ridgepole). Then Gallagher stepped up behind her, between her feet, unbuttoned his fly, and eased out his cock. He leaned on her hard, James, rubbing himself up a fine hard-on, and slipped it into her. Then he commenced to fuck her, hard, pressing his big meaty hand into the middle of her back.

Gallagher and Jonesy started to grin and wanted to laugh, and a couple dudes *did* laugh, because no one in the company had had any pussy for a month of Sundays (except for Lieutenant Stennett, who hadn't been in this man's army that long).

And when Gallagher finished, Jonesy fucked her, and when Jonesy was done, half the fucking company was standing in line and commenced to fuck her ragged. The girl bit the inside of her cheek to keep back the rancor. The line of dudes crowded the low and narrow doorway, drinking bitterly sour canteen water and the warm beers they'd been saving, smoking cigars and jays, and watching one another while they ground the girl into the rubble. Her eyes got bigger than a deer's, and the chunks and slivers of tile got ground into her scalp and face, her breasts and stomach, and Jesus-fucking-Christ, she had her nostrils flared and teeth clenched and eyes squinted, tearing at the sheer humiliating, grinding pain of it. (Paco remembers feeling her whole body pucker down; feels her bowels, right here and now, squeezing as tight as if you were ringing out a rag, James; can see the huge red mark in the middle of her back; hears her involuntarily snorting and spitting; can see the broad smudge of blood on the table as clear as day; hears all those dudes walking on all that rubble.) Dudes still ambled over to the doorway to watch, to call out coaching, taking their turns, hanging around the side of the building after— some getting back in line.

And clean across the clearing—way the hell on the other side of the laager; way the fuck out in left field on the other side of the moon—Lieutenant Stennett squatted on his steel pot with his knees up and his back to the doings in the hooch, making himself a canteen cup of coffee. The dudes at the quiet end of the line heard the feathery hiss of the thumb-sized chunk of C–4 plastic explosive, and the clank of the green bamboo twig he stirred it with, but don't you know, James, we didn't pay it so much as a never-you-mind. The lieutenant heard the grinding, raucous laughter behind him; heard that raw-wood table squeak and creak, creeping across the floor, shoved at and shoved at the way you might pound at a kitchen table with the heel of your hand. And if he'd had a mind to, he could have glanced back over his shoulder and seen that line and that bit of commo wire looped over the mahogany ridgepole. He knew what was what in that hooch all right, all right—he might have been a fool, James, but he wasn't a *stone* fool. He worked his shoulders, trying to ease that damp, raw-boned, sticky-sweaty feeling of sleep out of his back. He kept his back and his head slumped, tending his hissing little C–4 fire, stirring the caked and lumpy thousand-year-old C-ration instant coffee furiously with a knotted bamboo stick until you'd have thought he was going to wear a hole in it, if you didn't know better; studying it like it might be entrails.

And when everyone had had as many turns as he wanted (Paco fascinated by the huge red welt in the middle of her back), as many turns as he could stand, Gallagher took the girl out behind that bullshit brick-and-stucco hooch, yanking her this way and that by the whole head of her hair (later that afternoon we noticed black hairs on the back of his arm). He had a hold of her the way you'd grab some shrimpy little fucker by the throat—motherfuck-you-up street-mean and businesslike—and he slammed her against the wall and hoisted her up until her gnarled toes barely touched the ground. But the girl didn't much fucking care, James. There was spit and snot, blood and drool and cum all over her, and she'd pissed herself. Her eyes had that dead, clammy glare to them, and she didn't seem to know what was happening anymore. Gallagher slipped his .357 Magnum out of its holster and leaned the barrel deftly against her breastbone. "We gonna play us a little game. We gonna play tag," he said in a clear and resonant voice, "but who's it?" he said, and jerked the girl once, and her eyes snapped. "Who's it? Why, you are, Sweet Pea."

Then he put the muzzle of the pistol to her forehead, between her eyebrows. He held her up stiffly by the hair and worked his finger on it, to get a good grip (a .357 ain't some chickenshit, metal-shop, hand-crank zip gun, James). The girl glared at the red-and-black tattoo of the dragon, and she was almost near enough to his hand to purse her lips and kiss his knuckles. And then in the middle of us jostling and grab-assing, Gallagher squeezed off a round. Boom.

The pistol bucked and Gallagher's whole body shimmered with the concussion; we all eyed him quickly. Some of the fucking new guys flinched, and Lieutenant Stennett positively jerked his arm and splashed himself with scalding coffee. Smoke rose from the pistol and Gallagher's hand in a cloud, in wisps. If you had listened closely, you would have heard the ring of metal on metal, the same as you hear a 105 howitzer ring with that *tang* sound; a sound the same as if you had hauled off and whacked a 30-foot I beam with a 10-pound ballpeen—a sound you feel in every bone of your body from the marrow out.

Her head was so close to the hooch that we heard the shot simultaneously with the clack and clatter of bone chips against the brick and stucco. The pistol slug and the hard, splintered chips of brick ricocheted and struck her in the meatiest part of her back, between her shoulder blades. Just that quick there was blood all over everything and everyone, and splinters of bone and brick stuck to our clothes and the bare skin of our arms and faces. And the girl was dead in that instant (and we mean *stone* dead, James) and lay in her own abundant blood. Her hands and arms fluttered the same as a dog's when it dreams.

Paco remembers the spray of blood, the splatter of brick and bone chips on Gallagher and Jonesy and *every*one, as thick as freckles, and how it sparkled. He remembers that quick, tingling itch of the spray, like a mist of rain blown through a porch screen. He remembers the brown bloodstains down the fronts of our trousers for days afterward; remembers Gallagher turning to the rest of us, still holding her scalp, and how we made a path for him when he walked away, hearing him say out loud (the timbre and resonance of his voice reverberating superbly), as if we were in an auditorium, *"That's* how you put the cool on gooks."

Some of us shook out of our reverie and walked away, too, but the rest lingered with resentful and curious fascination, staring down at the bloody, filthy bottoms of her feet, her slumped head and flat, mannish face. The whole expression of her body was drawn to the dry, drooping lips and lolling tongue. We looked at her and at ourselves, drawing breath again and again, and knew that this was a moment of evil, that we would never live the same. It even began to dawn on Lieutenant Stennett, the English major from Dartmouth, who'd been sitting pucker-assed on the other side of the night laager with his back as round and smooth as a beach pebble, still stirring his C-ration coffee and minding his Ps and Qs like there was no tomorrow. Good morning to you, Lieutenant. Ain't you got that coffee fried yet?

Soon enough, we heard the thump-thump-thump, whomp-whomp-whomp of the dust-off chopper come to pick up the KIAs. It circled the laager once, coming around upwind, and landed in the middle of the hooch yard. One by one we backed away from the girl's corpse and went to help load the body bags, and by that time the girl—whatever her name was —was still. When the chopper was loaded, it rose and left. Lieutenant Stennett got word from Colonel Hubbel for us to hit the road for Fire Base Carolyne. We finished breakfast, saddled up our rucksacks, turned our backs to that hooch, and left that place—we never went back. Perhaps the girl's body was found later, and buried, but we would never know.

Paco sprawls spread-eagle on his bed in his one-room room, itchy hot and stinking drunk, thinking about Gallagher's red-and-black tattoo and the girl and the rape, and that look the dust-off medics gave us.

There is nothing to do for the squeeze-you-down heat but lie still—it is too oppressive for anything else. Cathy and Marty-boy are still fucking up a storm an arm's length away, their bodies slapping together, Cathy sighing contentedly. Paco's cock is still iron hard and his groin aches—he cannot help his hard-on. And when they finish Cathy says in an exhausted wine-drunk voice, "Oh, Marty-boy, that was just super!" Marty-boy pours the last of their warm Roditys richly into his plastic cold-drink cup, and Paco hears the pat of dry bare feet on the cheap carpet as they share from the cup. Marty-boy stands among the pretzel crumbs and old wine spills, easy and quiet, feeling the bit of cool of the dark drift in the tall front windows, then hustles into his pants, the loose change jangling and his keys rattling. He cinches his belt and ties his sneakers, all the while looking at Cathy lazily rolling and curling this way and that—her beautiful body glistening —cuddling herself. Paco hears Marty-boy leave her rooms, step gingerly down the stairway and out the front door of the hotel, easing the screen door back in its jamb (gleaming at his own cleverness). Paco hears him walk down the middle of the street past the Texas Lunch, scuffing the pavement along the dashed white center line as he goes.

Cathy lounges on her bed, murmuring. Paco lies on his bed with his eyes closed, but awake, daydreaming, brushing the fuzzy wallpaper with the back of his hand and waiting for first light, the coolest part of the day.

7. Paco the Sneak. The very next night—Friday, as it happens, James—Paco comes home from work, opens his door, turns on the light, and has the immediate sense that someone has been in the room. Standing in the doorway and leaning on his cane, as tired as he is, he scans the piles of unfolded laundry, the unmade bed, the scatter of knickknacks and oddments on top of the bureau (including that petri dish of shrapnel and rifle slugs and bone fragments as thin as fish hooks). But, too, there is an odor that he cannot place— perfume? The smell of different clothes? Ordinary body odor? Something! Someone has been in my room, Paco thinks to himself. A handprint on the brown enamel bedstead; a drawer not slipped back far enough in its slide; something has been picked up and looked at and not put back just right. (And, James, don't you know the only person he can think of is Cathy, the prick tease, from down the hall.)

The next morning, Saturday, he wakens in the full light of day, his back turned to the window, hearing a softball game in the park by the river behind Hennig's Barbershop and across from Rita's Tender Tap—the infielders razzing the batter:

> *Hey, batta-batta-batta, SWING!*
> *This guy can't hit!*
> *This guy can't hit!*
> *Come on, ya cripple, SWING!*

The infielders hop from one foot to the other, clapping and teasing; the pitcher faking underhand pitches:

> *Easy out! Easy out!*
> *This guy can't hit!*
> *SWING, you gimp!*
> *Aw, COME ON, you swing like a girl!*
> *This cripple can't hit!*
> *Hey, batta-batta-batta, SWING!*

Then Paco hears Cathy and Marty-boy leave her apartment (the two of them dressed for a hot day's traveling; Cathy in one of her famous, low-cut, summery "come-fuck-me" dresses); her door clicked closed. Paco listens, lying on his back, to the blur of noise downstairs—Earl and Myrna eating breakfast at the bar and watching an old Dan Dailey– James Cagney movie; Cathy telling her aunt and uncle that she and Marty-boy are going to visit her folks and will be back Sunday night; Myrna taking one good look at that dress and thinking to herself, *Sure*, but why does it have to be Martin Hubbard? Paco hears them getting into Marty-boy's rusted-out beater of a Mustang, and a shrewd look comes into his large brown eyes as the Mustang revs and leaves—he can jimmy his way into Cathy's room and see what's what with her. The softball game roars up again, the players throwing down their gloves to dispute a tagged slide (standing in the deep dust of the batting grooves around home plate—"You only *think* you got him," says one guy. "Aw, *bullshit*, I heard the fuckin' leather slap his side, son-of-a-bitch. For Christ's sake," says the guy coming in from shortstop and pointing to the first guy with all his fingers, "fuck you and the horse you rode in on. Tough shit, bub, a tag's a tag . . .").

All that long Saturday at work Paco is preoccupied about what he's going to find in Cathy's apartment—brooding. And that night he goes straight up to bed despite the noise in the bar downstairs, goes right to sleep.

He wakes toward morning as the low horizon is just brightening to gray. In one swift and efficient motion he rises, then slips on a dark T-shirt and a pair of cutoff dungarees (scrubbed to death and plenty salty-looking, the cuffs tangled with bleached threads)—the fewer the clothes, James, the less the noise—and carefully opens his door and slips out into the hall. He leaves his door open, just in case (always trust your luck, James, but why push your luck), and stands sideways for the longest time, barefoot, to accustom himself to the light. He intently eyes the corner of the hallway and the stairway railing across the way from Cathy's room. He sidesteps down the hall, the runway carpet as smooth as sun-warmed yard dirt, the wallpaper rough as driveway concrete against his arms and shoulders. He stands next to the railing above the stairwell, casual and alert (the air of the stairs smelling of grimy old age), listening down into the dining room and bar for as little a thing as someone winding a watch, hearing only the deep, solid ticking of the old Regulator pendulum clock downstairs next to the pay-phone booth. The porch chairs out front bob and rattle against one another with any fresh breath of air; the dining-room fan blades *ting* against the bent wire mesh as the early-morning air moves into the place and up the stairs. Paco stands next to the railing inexorable and calm, feeling as though his mind has expanded to become the hotel itself—so plainly and keenly does he hear the shushing of the fan and the bobbing of the chairs and the hush of air as it rises up the stairs (and the water pouring over the spillway, under the bridge down the street). Paco eases along the mahogany railing and slides to the head of the stairs; he stops again and listens more. Not a peep—everyone is still. He takes those three paces to Cathy's door and stands before it with an ear cocked, poised on the balls of his feet, listening fiercely through the loose jamb. Then he glances sidelong behind him, down through the railing rungs, from the vantage point where Cathy usually stands in the doorway, staring at him, teasing, when he comes into the hotel from work. He tries to imagine himself standing at the foot of the stairs next to the phone booth, sweaty-filthy, stinking from work, leaning on his black hickory cane—half drunk some nights, his back always killing him, tired as hell.

Now, James, if Gallagher was the company killer and the company clown, proud of both that famous Zippo lighter of his and the red-and-black Bangkok R & R tattoo, whose mood swings would physic a woodpecker and had fretted Lieutenant Stennett to distraction; and if Pfc. Lester, the guy who tape-recorded all our firefights, volunteered for sharp-shooter school (to get out of the field) and returned three weeks later with an M–14 with scope and carrying case, and a $1,000 pair of artillery field glasses—the company sniper who could draw a bead on a VC (man, woman, or child) and drop them in their tracks at 500 meters and more, so they never knew what hit them; and if the 3rd platoon's permanent ambush patrol was four dufus-looking guys everyone called Huey, Dewey, and Louie, plus Dorothy from Kansas, each one more gawky and cross-eyed and dipstick-looking than the one before, and who avoided contact like a bad smell; then Paco was the company booby-trap man, who knew when and where to set them (in rows or in clusters, up and down likely avenues of approach, to enhance fields of fire—down a ravine, say, or under a likely sniper position), and seemed to know the tensile strength of half a dozen kinds of wire.

For instance, we'd arrive at Fire Base Harriette and move in among the bunkers and gun positions heavily fortified with thick timbers and plenty of sandbags—everything connected by elaborate, chest-high trenches. From overhead Fire Base Harriette looked like the cap of a cheap pepper shaker, you understand; every swinging dick in the company knew that Harriette was a piece of cake. After a hearty supper Lieutenant Stennett would call Colonel Hubbel from his command bunker at the crest of the rise and report happily that there was nothing to report, and that he—Lieutenant Stennett—was setting the guard, sending out the night listening posts (LPs, we called them) and the ambushes (Huey, Dewey, and Louie, plus Dorothy from Kansas, on a north-north by west azimuth 1,500 meters into the Goongone Forest). Lieutenant Stennett would wish the colonel a good evening, motion the patrols to depart, loosen his bootlaces, and retire—lying back and pulling his poncho liner to his chin, soon to be fast asleep.

The rest of the company—us grunts—would clean our rifles and whatnot, swabbing them with oil-soaked shaving brushes; then we'd lay our bedrolls on the ground behind the trenchline, smoke a mess of dope to mellow down, loosen our bootlaces, and turn in, watching the stars come out and shooting the shit, feeling the serious gloom of the woods settling over us and the solid chill of the bare ground seeping into our backs—our legs looking like the many spokes of a wheel, our heads toward the hub.

But Paco would begin the evening at dusk by arraying his booby traps before him—tricked-up claymores, short-fused frags on stakes or in C-ration cans or rigged to tripflares (a magnesium flare would throw gobs of sparks everywhere and hiss like crazy, smoking like an orchard smudge pot), C–4 shaped charges spiked with nails and scrap iron scrounged from the engineers; a roll of OD gaffers tape, wire cutters, a small crimping tool, a bundle of long slivers of bamboo (punji stakes), and a number of spools of blackened wire—all that as well as his 6-inch Chicago Cutlery fillet knife and Lester's .45 borrowed for the night. Paco would select a number of booby traps, cram them into a gray gas-mask bag he had, secure it tightly around the small of his back, slip the fillet knife under the strap around his belly, then wait for dark and crawl on his hands and knees from the edge of the perimeter into the woods. Gallagher and Jonesy and Jigs, the medic, and some of the rest of us would lie back, smoking our dope and drinking spiked canteens fetched from the village out by the road, waiting up for him. And hours later the bunker guards would hear a distinct and audible hiss. "Psst! Hey!" Paco would whisper. The guards would rouse and stretch, and wave him in. And he'd come back from these sorties low-crawling on his belly, as easy and quiet and sly as a snake slipping over a flat rock, using his elbows and the points of his hips—that gray gas-mask bag collapsed and flimsy, the fillet knife stuck in his back pocket like a spare screwdriver, holding Lester's .45 at the ready. He would sneak straight into the trenchline and make his way to his bedroll, crouching, and settle his gear. He would drink canteen after canteen of water, the sweat pouring down his face: "Mighty dry work, Jack!" he'd say, and laugh some and loosen his boots. Then he would smoke a mess of dope and drink a mess of booze, finally able to sleep.

And every once in a great while, in the middle of the night we'd hear a solid *whomp* in the woods, a flash of light like a quick spark (at Fire Base Francesca or Carolyne, too—the whole company astonished how close to the perimeter it was), and everyone would know that one of Paco's booby traps had suckered some zip—the smoke rising through the jungle canopy like a snuffed campfire. Lieutenant Stennett would get all fidgety and sly, low-crawling over to Paco, and want to wake him—the man curled up on the ground in his poncho liner with the power to kill another man, unseen, and still sleep profoundly, when the suspense was sweating the rest of us rag-limp. Lieutenant Stennett never did have the gumption to rouse him—guys do funny things when you snap them out of a sound sleep in the middle of the night in the field, James.

Anyway, Paco always said that you could pretty much tell if you got a kill or just a hit by how solid the *whomp* was.

(Let us understand from the very first, James, that booby traps—known as mechanical ambushes—are clearly illegal

and expressly forbidden according to the Geneva Convention
Rules of War, and to use them is a war crime, the same as
slave labor, the torture and execution of prisoners, the use of
chemical-biological weapons, snipers, and such as that. How-
ever, the zips used booby traps—huge and elaborate, bloody
and nasty businesslike machines—and since what is sauce for
the goose is sauce for the gander, everyone used them; "What
the fuck," Paco would say, taping a short-fused frag and a
stick of C-4 to a punji stake with his OD gaffers tape, "better
motherfuckin' safe than motherfuckin' sorry, *right*?")

One time on a night laager near Fire Base Francesca,
Paco low-crawled out onto a hard-packed footpath that was
not much more than a dip in the turf—it came from a hamlet
of three hooches and wound through a thick bamboo grove
—a man had to walk well stooped over and put one foot in
front of the other as if the path were a log over a creek. Paco
lay on his stomach. The dew-wet turf felt prickly; the dirt
path—not any wider than the spread of your hand, James—
felt as sticky and tacky as a raw pike fillet gone bad. He was
finishing the last of a string of tricked frags, the damp cool
of the dirt seeping into his crotch and belly as he worked the
last wire taut—a tight wire is harder to see, for some reason.
Then he heard an unmistakable hush in the woods, a harsh
muffled whisper, the tappety-tap clatter of the bamboo, the
soft brush of metal through foliage. And in an instant his
whole body tightened and tingled; he smelled the greasy, foul-
water stink of Viets living a long time in the jungle, coming
up the path. He judged another twenty paces and whoever it
was would be upon him, stepping on his back. Immediately he
set down his work and picked up a spare frag, gripping it
tightly, and quickly pulled the pin, holding down the spoon,

but ready to chuck it as far as he could. Then he felt in the grass for Lester's .45, slipped the safety off—seven rounds in the magazine and one in the chamber. Lying on his belly, he tossed the frag—like shoveling off a forward pass; the thing carooming down the dirt path like an egg—ducked his head behind his arms, and counted off the fuse time: One-thousand-one, one-thousand-two, one-thousand-three, one-thousand-four, one-thou—; then *whomp*, that quick spark, the zip hit hard and blown back—all that shrapnel in his eyes and down his front. The zip rolled around as if he'd been kicked, setting off a fine clatter among the bamboo, holding his face tightly—blinded, screaming bloody murder; Paco thinking, That's just fine, now every zip in the township is going to know we're here. He slipped the .45 under his belt at the small of his back, pulling his fillet knife out, and crawled carefully forward, feeling for the booby-trap tripwires in the dark with delicately scrabbling fingers, disarming each booby trap as he came to it as smoothly and neatly as you'd close a big scissors. A long time it took Paco to reach him, the guy squirming and whining as though horribly scalded. Paco found with his fingers the place where the frag went off (the bare dirt rough as rawhide) and quickly made out the guy's feet and legs, the guy himself slashed open in a hundred places like a burst plum—split open (the memory of the choking smell of the blood-clotted gore making Paco gag; him standing at the corner of the hallway across the stairwell from Cathy's room, listening down the stairs). Then Paco grabbed the zip by the whole of the front of his shirt, slamming him into the dirt of the path so that he grunted like a fat old cat jumping down from your lap. He had the guy and held him. He felt the guy's chest for the space between the fourth and fifth ribs on the left side, and then took his Chicago Cutlery fillet knife and insinuated it there, first pricking the skin, then stabbing down firmly—like cutting into a hard, warm cheese. They both heard the flat of the blade slice down between the bones. The guy gasped and wiggled, fighting. Paco, holding him by the shirt with a knee in his groin, worked the knife into the guy's heart (the strongest muscle in your body, you understand), piercing directly into the left ventricle. The guy sucked air through his gaping mouth—as if that long breath would somehow assuage the incredible, gripping pain and keep it at bay—the air hissing through his teeth as he gasped (the knife keenly burning). The heart muscle jerked the knife in Paco's grip, blood bubbling up furiously into his hand and filling the cavity of the guy's chest and up into his neck; everything turning a deep bruise color. Paco pushed the clean carbide blade. The man gasped as if the wind were knocked out of him and he was trying to recover, but he whispered distinctly in up-country Viet, *"Lạy ông xin đừng giết tôi. Trời ởi! Xin đừng làm vây."* ("I pray you, please don't kill me. Oh, God! Please do not do this, I beg you" is a decent translation, James.) He looked up at Paco man-to-man—the overpowering, stinging pain welling up in him, overwhelming him; Please, he said, as if talking to his older brother and relying on a lifetime's blood relations, *please* do not do this. Paco held him firmly, one knee in the guy's groin. Blood welled up through the knife slit into Paco's fisted grip: Paco felt the desperate clutch of the guy's heart; felt the twitches of pulse in his hand and up his sweaty arm. The plain wooden handle of the fillet knife was sloppy with blood, jerking.

"*Chết tôi rồi,*" the guy said ("I am dead already")—fainting from shock; very soon to be dead, Paco knew—whispering with a dry mouth but in a clear voice. The guy breathed, breathed again, again, and then he came to his last breath; the tension in his body released and his face went slack—dead.

Paco straightened the knife in the slit and drew it out, his grip slippery with blood.

Later, after Paco had cleaned up, dragged the guy's body into the bamboo and set booby traps around it, gathered up his gear, and come back to the night laager, he told Gallagher and Jonesy and some of the rest of us what had happened. He sat on his bedroll, drinking canteen after canteen of water, and talked in hissing whispers. His face shined as though greased with a foul, viscous wax, and the fierce glare of his 1,000-meter stare seemed permanent—his concentration deep (Paco's ears ringing, his heart pounding; the tepid water cold going down his throat), his whole body skittish—Paco always able to recall the tears in the guy's eyes while he whispered clearly and plainly, "Vĩnh biệt. Vĩnh biệt. Vĩnh biệt." ("I will never see forever.") That night he drank every canteen in sight and smoked dope until he was high out of his mind.

At first light Lieutenant Stennett sent out a patrol to see just what there was to see, and we found the zip—festooned with booby traps, we knew, lying in a pool of his own blood as big as a bedspread, flies in his face—Gallagher taking plenty of pictures.

Paco stands in front of Cathy's door (the large numeral 5 painted over with many coats of cheap varnish like so much dried mud), palms up and head cocked, listening acutely into the room with his ear not quite against the door—his hands pressed delicately to the woodwork, as if to help with the listening—for any telltale that Cathy might have come home early. Then he slips his own brass skeleton key into the lock, takes hold of the porcelain knob (the whole sorry antique mechanism worn and sloppy), and slowly turns the slack out of it, as if he were fine-tuning a carburetor. Then with a quiet bit of fooling he jimmies it, feeling the latch give way, and the door (warped on its hinges) springs open a hairsbreadth with a quick *snip*, like the click of a bar tap. (Oh ho, Mr. Rabbit, Paco thinks to himself, repeating a line from an old folktale.)

And so in he goes, careful to lock the door behind him. It will soon be dawn, James, but the burnt-orange light does not occupy the eastern horizon by the width of a hand.

Cathy's apartment is hot and stuffy (with the windows closed and locked), smells of expensive cologne, and is as neat as a pin. The front room, with those three tall windows on the street, is about as cool as it's going to be on such a stifling-hot, late-summer Sunday. Her sheer drapes hang straight down in front of thick paper shades (pulled almost to the floor)—the shades water-spotted antiques with long, curling edges, as brown as old newsprint. And as early as it is, the room already glows with an aged amber light; the atmosphere is like a straitjacket. Paco stands in the buttery-warm light, barefoot, calmly eyeing the room, and an exquisite stillness settles over him—almost an ambush trance (that blunt and slow-motion, self-destructive death wish); a grim shiver of anticipation ripples through his feet and fingers; the hair bristles at the back of his neck and behind his ears; his back hardens; his look hardens—glistens—and his eyes sparkle. He feels enveloped in an alien ease (and us with him, James), as if he's been turned inside out and rendered invisible.

Paco glides into Cathy's bedroom—bedcovers as smooth as a barracks bunk and lined with many small, fringed pillows; a big, old, uncomfortable-looking rocking chair next to the bed, a tall reading lamp in between. The high bureau against the wall is covered with a long linen coverlet embroidered with pinkish edelweiss and banners of holly. A fragrant pink talc is spilled all over her brush and comb (blond hair tangled there as big as your fist) and the junk trinkets in her white wicker jewelry box. Half a dozen plain cotton brassieres (the cups smeared with rouge) and skimpy bikini tops hang from the fancy hinges of the bureau mirror and the back of the rocking chair. He fingers through her dresser drawers, pawing the rest of the helter-skelter underwear, thumbing the blouses and striped tube tops, the tennis shorts and summer sweaters. He flips through her other summer dresses hanging in an improvised cardboard closet. He runs his hands purposefully under her mattress (smelling richly of Cathy and Marty-boy's fucking, her strong cologne, stale reefer, and that pink talc). At last he finds her diary, a burlap-bound, ledger-looking affair about the size of a good book and (Paco checking quickly) about two-thirds finished.

He stands at the foot of her bed with the grainy burlap diary under his arm, and can easily see out her window into his own room—dirty work clothes under the chair, black hickory cane hanging on a hook back of the door, the unmade bed.

Some nights Cathy would sit slouched in the dark, James, across the foot of her bed, and watch Paco in his room with that diary on her knee—Paco's eyes shining in the moonlit dark (the ache of his wounds at such times stirring him deeply; his craving for medication urgent and everlasting).

Cathy would ponder the tight, dark bulge in his crotch and the endless mosaic, the wonder, of all those scars, while she scribbled notes and strummed her 14k gold anklet.

The lights of the sign in front of Cathy's rooms blink and click; the steady, far-off hush of the river pouring over the spillway at the end of the street roars up into Paco's ears. He swings into the bathroom to pour himself a beer mug of water—Cathy's simple array of cosmetics laid out on a towel on the toilet tank. He circles back into the buttery-warm light of the living room, pulls out the chair Cathy sits in (slouched slightly) when she spies on Paco working (leaning into his work with his belt buckle hooked over the edge of the wash-tub). He sits down and tips back against the arm of her old swayback couch, putting his feet up on her writing desk—a big old manila-wood teacher's desk with a large kraft-paper blotter, a Sears, Roebuck Smith-Corona typewriter, one of those cheap banker's lamps with a green glass shade, and a ceramic flower vase in the shape of a perched squirrel (stuffed with plenty of pencils).

Paco would often see Cathy from the back stoop of the Texas Lunch sitting at her desk with her back to the window —writing in this diary, he now supposes; crossing his ankles and getting comfortable—in her plain, threadbare underwear or fresh from the shower with a country-club towel wrapped around her, shaking her head vigorously to dry her hair (Paco watching the flying droplets sparkle). She would sit there with her diary spread flat on the desk in front of her, holding a dark-leaded pencil with nearly all her fingertips—her nails white and her hand cramped—cheating with a piece of heavily lined cardboard under the page. Her script was bright and neat, and as small as the nub of soft lead would allow (she sharpened her pencils with a workman's penknife, a habit got from her architect father, the graphite already beginning to fade from the earliest entries). And sometimes she would spread out on the swayback, old couch, with her back to a tall, ugly lamp she draped with a peach-colored shawl to soften its harsh glare—Cathy up half the night reading and writing in her diary, with all the windows open and the floor fan going full-blast, oblivious to the heat as if she were impervious to it.

Paco sets his mug on the floor—a ring of water forming quickly—and opens the diary, careful not to crack the binding (though Cathy breaks it back for every page she turns, then smoothing the pages down with her hand). The diary is almost a year old, a going-away present from her mother ("It's time you started keeping track of things that are important to you," her mother told her), and Paco skims through it, a page here and a page there:

I have a "suite," no less . . . Dad calls Earl, Mom's brother-in-law, a little loopy for buying this dump. Calls Myrna a dingbat. The place was built in 1904, which is certainly true by the smell of the woodwork and the linoleum. But the rent is right, brother . . .

Thanksgiving was *another* disaster. Frank brought home his dumbshit girlfriend, Virginia Crowley. She is very pretty. I will own to that. And as Frank says, quote, Built like a brick shithouse, unquote. (So eloquent, Frank is.) Which is apparently a very important aspect of her personality. But she is as dumb as a stump. They've been sleeping together for a year I know of. Anyway, there

I was at Thanksgiving. And I am supposed to sit at the dinner table, composed and polite, and eat my dinner with a straight face and be thankful with a capital *T*. That slob spilled gravy in her wine, dropped a Haviland china serving bowl of sweet potatoes on her plate. "My, that's hot!" she said, and blew on her fingers as if she'd been bit. Oh, my aching back, Virginia, save the act for the movies. And through the whole meal, meanwhile, she's making eyes at Dad and playing footies with Frank. Honestly, I wanted to say to Frank, "Don't you get enough of that in bed?"

After dinner, after dessert and all, I'd had about all I could take, so I took the car over to Muriel's and we played cutthroat hearts until 4.

Got a note about which present I should get Mom for Christmas. That Italian suit we saw at Walther's, and a subscription to *Arizona Highways* for a "gag."

All those guys staring at me. The men teachers, too. Makes me feel like a piece of meat. When I walk across the campus what is it they imagine under the ski jacket and sweater, not to mention the armful of books, but I figure I've got the pick of this litter. And his name is Martin Hubbard. He stares plenty hard, too, but he's the one who'll be getting an eyeful soon enough.

Marty-boy, Lynette calls him. But she doesn't fuck, so she's not any competition . . .

Paco looks up from the diary and has to laugh to himself; he glances over his shoulder into her bedroom, where the rouged bras hang on the mirror, and his groin stirs. He lets a couple of pages slip past his fingers, reaches down for a drink of water, then reads:

. . . and she tells me behind her hand (Fuller is diagramming frogs' guts) there is a good-looking guy working at the Texas Lunch. I bicycle home and hop across the street for coffee and a good look. Well, hell's bells, you could have knocked me over with a feather. It's the guy who lives down the hall here. And he is good-looking, with nice tight buns. He's circling around the place, jerking bus pans and hauling them to the back.

. . . with June from theory class. And we're sitting there with our coffee and out he comes with stacks of dishes. And he's cute, you know, but covered with scars. Wounded in the war, Unc says. Scars everywhere. But wouldn't that be something to tell my grand-children, sleeping with two guys at once.

Paco well remembers Cathy and her girlfriends coming into the Texas Lunch, afternoons, with their books and bags, drinking coffee and horsing around until the first of the din-ner hour. And it seemed odd (even Ernest remarked how odd it was), because that summer-session college crowd didn't much bother with the Texas Lunch regulars—though they'd cruise in late on a weekend night (Big Buddy out rousting lovers necking and fucking along the forest preserve roads; the only kicks the fat man got), six or seven sheets to the wind, these guys, hanging around pale and sloppy drunk, try-ing to sober up enough to get back into the dorm before curfew. *These* college guys never got laid, mind you, James.

And every once in a while one of them would get this dia-
bolically funny look on his face, jump up, and run out back
to throw up all over the alley ("Boo-wah! Boo-wah!"); sometimes they'd run relays and sometimes they'd go in a gang,
acting as if it were a contest—who could barf the loudest or
the ugliest or the highest on the hardware-store wall. And Paco
would stand at his back sink, grim with pain, watching the
parade—those guys smelling of cheap, fishing-trip beer—and
he'd laugh right out loud in their faces, thinking, Hey, dipstick,
if you can't drink it good enough to keep it down, don't drink
it down. Ain't there any of these college guys got their head
out their ass?

(Tell you what, James, if there was one thing we learned
in the Army—along with everything else—it was how to drink
any kind of liquor we could get the top off of, and how to *hold*
our liquor.)

Paco, flipping through Cathy's diary some more, reads:

It's real late. Marty-boy came up to my room tonight. I finally
snuck him past Unc, though I'm sure Aunt Myrna knows. She keeps
the books around here as well as keeping house, and keeps pretty
close tabs on me, so nothing much gets past her.

(Cathy sat at her desk, naked, on a towel, sipping whiskey-
and-water with plenty of ice from her beer mug, still wet from
their fucking and the back of her neck splashed with cologne.)

A couple of days ago she asked me if I used the pill, had a dia-
phragm, knew about rubbers. *Prophylactics* was the word she used.

Yes, Aunt Myrna. What kind of fool do you take me for, Aunt Myrna? Breathing all the time, Aunt Myrna.

Marty-boy is asleep on the couch behind me. I made him wait while I went and put on my raspberry baby-doll. Without the panties. And, good little boy that he is, he just *stared* at my breasts. I get a buzz between my legs just thinking about the look on his face. All these guys are run by their glands and organs. I'll give Marty-boy credit for one thing, though. He's got a nice body and a nice cock. Not as good-looking as that guy Paco, but it'll do. Reminds me of one of those hollow yellow pencils where you kept your pens and pencils when you were in 2nd/3rd grade. Well, Marty-boy's cock is like that, only smaller. And I'll give his fucks a 7. And what's fun is that he'll do anything I ask. Isn't that what Dad says about the Marines? Go anywhere and do anything.

Paco sits forward, letting the chair right itself—"Is *that* what they say about Marines?" he mutters to himself, and wants to laugh out loud. *Anything*? he thinks. *Any*-where?—what was it that Gallagher used to say: " 'Anything' sure does cover a lot of law, Jack!" Paco leans back in the chair again and flips on through the diary, the script switching to a plain and squarish block print done with a ball-point pen. (It was easier for Cathy to print with her diary in her lap—legs up and toes shoved down between the cushions.) Paco reads:

He comes into his room and hangs his cane on a dresser knob. He peels off his T-shirt, really struggling some nights and when he holds it in his hand it looks like a gray sodden rag. He washes his face and chest in a basin. And those scars. Look like purple and brown and white swirls, deep, and pinched together here and there like the heavy stitches of a quilt. He keeps two big bottles of pills on his dresser. Unc says they're VA prescriptions, but you have to wonder. And sometimes he'll have a pint or more of Thunderbird vodka or Mogen David 20/20 from the package counter downstairs.

(Cathy sat writing, and paused to take a sip of watered whiskey, well able to remember the medicinal smell of that cheap booze—" 'Mad Dog 20/20,' Unc called it." She looked down around behind her, across the street and in the back door of the Texas Lunch, hearing the cacophony of Paco as he shuffled dishes together on the drain-dry rack; Paco wiping the pouring sweat on the short sleeve of his T-shirt with every other breath, rubbing his face raw, James.)

He'll take a couple of pills and a drink from his bottle, then sit down and untie his shoes. The laces and leather squeak. Then he takes down his jeans or wash pants and throws *every*thing under his chair. And lies on the bed in his underwear, or naked, now that the weather's hotter and hotter, talking to himself and rubbing his pasty, wrinkly feet together. And sometimes he prances around, but kind of hobbling, kind of deeply and slowly limping. He's got the pills and that bottle on the dresser. Getting more and more drunk, holding his head with both hands. Slapping the flat of his belly with cupped hands, making a POP POP POP sound. Hoarsely whispering, "Come on, hit me! Hit me! Hit me!" and taking time out to wave that bottle around, drinking and splashing booze and slurring, "Bang! Bang! Bang-bang-bang!" Flicking his wrist and sprinkling booze in all the corners of his room.

And his room is so depressing. Faded wallpaper, no telling what the motif was, and that tacky, shabby linoleum, and he's a dingy, dreary, smelly, shabby, *shabby* little man.

Being ugly sure beats the shit out of being dead, Paco says out loud—suddenly craving some of that Mad Dog in his room—and flips toward the back of Cathy's writing:

He gives me the creeps. He has such a dogged way of working. He gets up in the morning, dresses. Clean, dirty, it's all the same to him. Goes straight to work, doesn't talk much with anyone. He gets this set look on his face. Gives me the creeps. Unc says he wonders if the guy knows where he is half the time. He'll sneak back across the street in the afternoon and have himself a drink.

Paco coming into the bar and making a bet that he can drink a shot of schnapps without using his hands. And, James, there's nearly always some sucker who'll ante up, just to see him perform.

Aunt Myrna says he has a way of stiffening up and staring right through you. As if he's a ghost. Or you're the ghost.

How could I have ever thought it might be fun to sleep with him? Unc says that creeps like him are best got rid of, and is going to start working on him . . .

. . . like for instance last night. It's real late and I can't sleep. I've got the floor fan going full-blast, reading Aunt Myrna's old copy of *Doctor Zhivago*. And this guy begins moaning and slamming back and forth on his bed. You know that real thick and solid sound of a mattress. And he's crying—weeping, I mean—"Oh no! Don't kill him!"

(Paco dreaming of the executions, James, standing with the flat of his shoulder blades against the ice-cold concrete wall, holding on to the guy in front of him as the medic in the lab coat stabbed him with the syringe and pushed the plunger. The man instantly dead, slipping out of Paco's hard grasp.)

. . . and then he jerks awake, pumped up and out of bed. And drinking the rest of his bottle. Better than half a pint by the sound of it.

Then he's back in bed, rubbing his back, moaning . . .

(Paco exhausted by the dream, James, tired and hot; his eyes burning with fatigue and head stinging with grief.)

. . . And he's all pasty. And crippled. And honest to God, ugly. Curled up on his bed like death warmed over. Like he was someone back from the dead. "I just want to sleep. Let me sleep," he was saying, like there were people in the room, or maybe he meant me. I hear him stretching his back, cracking the vertebrae. Then he draws his foot onto his lap and massages it. Cracking more joints. By then it's 3 o'clock in the morning and what this guy is doing to his body is obscene . . .

. . . and anyway, last night I had this dream and I just can't get it out of my mind.

(Cathy sat on the edge of her chair at her desk, drinking cold black coffee left in the pot downstairs from last night, thick and bitter in her mouth.)

Paco comes into my room with his cane. I'm in my terry-cloth robe. We stand in the doorway of the bedroom, kissing. He smells like apples, and his face is hard and warm. And his hands are hard and warm. And both of us are eager to get into bed. He pulls the knot out of my robe sash, and has his arms around me. I un-buckle his belt, undo his pants, and push them down. Those scars at his throat are livid. And then we're on the bed and everything. And then we're fucking. And I just can't bring myself to touch him, so I take hold of the bedstead bars. He's done, but still between my legs. He holds himself up, stiff-armed, and arches his back and reaches up to his forehead and begins by pinching the skin there, but he's working the skin loose, and then begins to peel the scars off as if they were a mask. It's as if he's unbuttoning the snaps of a jacket. Like you'd see someone pull up dried spaghetti from a kitchen table. He held the scars in his fist as if they were a spool of twine tangled in a terrible knot. I close my eyes and turn my head, and urge him off me with my hips—but I think now that he must have thought I wanted to fuck more.

He's holding me down with that hard belly of his, and lays the scars on my chest. It *burns* . . .

(Cathy touched her throat, swallowing hard.)

. . . and I think I hear *screams*, as if each scar is a scream, and I look up at him again and he's peeling the scars down his arm, like long peels of sunburned skin, brown and oniony. Then he's kneel-ing on my shoulders, like we used to when we'd give a kid pink belly and he's laying strings of those scars on my face, and I'm beginning to suffocate. Then he reaches both hands behind him, as if he's going to pull off a T-shirt, grabbing and pulling the scars off his back. And I could hear the stitches ripping. And he lays them across my breasts and belly—tingling and burning—lays them in my hair, wrapping them around my head, like a skull cap.